THE PREY

R. J DYSON

absolutelyunprofessional.com
Wadsworth, OH

to those torchbearers of truth sparking
fires in the wasteland

⬭ 1 Down by the River

"**W**ho's there? These hands are lethal weapons. Chambermaid? Don't say I didn't warn you!" The hair stood up on the back of Chih-ming's neck. Dropping the book he was carrying, tea spilled across the cover as it hit the dirt. He wasn't used to seeing anyone down by the river so early in the morning.

"Morning, Ming," the young man said. "Chambermaid?"

"Sheesh! It's just you, Nuzrene," Chih replied, taking a deep breath and wiping the tea dripping down the sides of the mug he managed to hold onto. "Yeah, well... it's a nickname Joanna and I gave the monitors we think are snooping around these woods."

The older student continued watching the dark river water flow by. Chih had only known him for a few months, but it was clear Nuzrene was careful with his words—willing to let silence sit in a conversation. "You really *have* been getting up early, haven't you? The sun's just sneaking up on us, and you've already made tea. You doing alright?"

"I was looking forward to drinking it too," he said, flashing a smile in the fog now creeping along the riverbank. "I guess I just like the sound of the river before the busyness of the day."

"Sort of like your time sneaking into the museum every night on a quiet compound?" There were few things about Compound 40 that Chih looked back on with warm memories, but his time alone in the library, scouring off-compound records, and surfing the chain behind Stream made the cut. Nuzrene had quickly figured out that Chihming was as much a man of quiet routine as he was willing to dive into an adventure.

"I hadn't thought about it like that," said Chih, wiping muck from the well-worn book. "But that makes a lot of sense. I'd been creeping into the museum since I was a Seeker. Seems a stretch of silence in the dark each day is part of my DNA now."

"I know what you mean," he replied, patting the stone beside him and inviting Chih to sit. "I was an Interpreter when C-21 fell. For years I would sneak off-site through an underground infrastructure tunnel designed for water lines and electrical systems. It ran beneath my dorm and at the end was a hatch in the middle of nowhere right next to an internet relay tower. I traveled the world through that tower."

"So you'd be an Applier now, or a graduating one anyhow… You know, if you were still at the compound." Chih sat down, placed the book on his lap, then set his mug on top of it. "What was it like? Your compound?"

Nuzrene looked upstream. Reaching into the thigh pocket of his khaki pants, he pulled out a small silver key. Without looking, he began to rotate it in between his fingers slowly. Chih waited patiently. He had learned you couldn't rush Nuzrene for an answer.

"My compound? Well, I wouldn't exactly call it *mine*," Nuzrene said, chuckling at the thought. "Someday, someone's going to write a comprehensive history of the rise and fall of the Anti-Libertas movement. I think future generations will be shocked by the evil utopian nightmare inflicted upon the world in the name of *good*." Watching the bank along the opposite side of the river, Nuzrene took another deep breath. When he had first escaped, the young Interpreter took every opportunity to talk about the horrors of compound life in the Middle East. Now, he only shared what seemed beneficial in helping other students make sense of life beyond the walls.

Chih took a sip of tea and then opened the book. It was a small book about the size of the tablet still strapped to his forearm. Thin with a hardcover, he had borrowed it from the director's house.

"Still working on those few lines? You know, from that ancient letter Heschel and Joanna found. One of the elders in town had a partial copy in his study, right?"

"Strange that there would be a few pages of the same old book, or letter, or whatever it is that we found on C-40 tucked away here in town," said Chih, shaking his head and thumbing through the ragged pages.

"With the glow always a step ahead, I'm not sure anything could surprise me," Nuzrene replied. "What seems like luck or coincidence often turns out to be some sort of guidance toward a presupposed outcome. An old sage I once met called it providence. Haven't found a solid definition of it on the chain yet. A few elders seem to have a good grasp of the concept."

Chih nodded, watching each yellowed page slip past his thumb. "This is the reason I'm here in the first place…I think," he said, running his fingers across the spine. "The reason the glow has partnered with me. I can't help but wonder if there's more to unlock in these pages. More hidden messages, ya know? More clues that'll get us back to Hesch? Not sure I deserve…."

"Deserve what?" asked Nuzrene.

"Nothing," he hastily replied. "Nothing…Just working out some thoughts after leaving the compound."

Nuzrene grabbed Chih's shoulder and nodded. Pushing down, he rose to his feet. His right leg slowed him down, but it hadn't stopped him. "If it's anything like the few passages we've been able to unlock from some of John's ancient compatriots, I have no doubt the glow will stir up more than you can imagine—though, in my experience, probably not what you'd expect."

Squeezing the small book with both hands, Chih nodded, smelled the cover, then shook his head. "Every morning, I come down here, sip tea, and translate another few words. I know I could read the English draft on the chain, the one you've already worked to decipher, but when I do it this way…I don't know…I believe part of the mystery is in the ancient language itself. That I have to earn it. Like the truth is guaranteed to be in those strange signs and symbols if I work at it long enough. It was the last time anyhow…and I don't want to miss it."

It was late summer. Mornings by the river were cool and peaceful, though still just as humid as they had been in the courtyard on his way to session one. While the air felt the same, time moved at a different pace in town. A change Chih was thankful for.

Since crawling out of the cold river with Joanna at that very same spot, he had continued to stand a little taller, attempting to live up to his namesake, at least as far as others could tell. On the inside, though, he was wrestling with a nasty creature—tangling with the nagging hiss of guilt that claimed he had sacrificed Hesch for his own safety. An idea virus working its way into his heart. But in the morning, during his time by the river, alone, with the little red book, and the ancient text within it, he felt relief.

The glow wasn't always visible, either. Not like it had become at C-40. And it seemed to burn a little less within him lately too. Mostly illuminating his time in the little red book. Yet he could still feel it toiling, as though preparing him for the moment he would be called on again.

Nuzrene stood back and watched Chih settle into place beside the river, open the book, and begin to absorb the text. He had done the same thing when he arrived in town. In the same spot. At the same time of day. It's where he began to make sense of the glow.

"I'll see you back in town, Chih." Turning to walk away, he caught a glimpse of the glow from Chih's eyes lighting up the page. Of all the ways he had witnessed the orb in town, Chih's eye-glow was a first. "And watch out for those Chambermaids."

⊙ 2 Socratic Parables

"**M**ing, I don't know how you can spend every morning down by the river working on those words," Joanna said as Chih entered the room. Smiling, he looked down at the little red book in his hand, then shrugged his shoulders.

"Why don't you join me tomorrow," he offered, "You'll see how peaceful it is down there."

Joanna's eyes grew wide, "Uhhh...ya know...um... would you look at that," she said, looking at her blank device, "I just realized I have plans around that time. Important things, ya know? Like planting ferns and watering trees...or something."

"Smooth, Joanna," said Nuzrene, watching from across

the room.

"Seriously though, how was it this morning?" Joanna asked, her tone shifting from playful to concerned. "Find anything? Hear anything? See anything?"

Chih shook his head. "Nah…it's hard to explain. I feel it sometimes. I feel the glow nudging me, ya know? I mean, I've only seen the orb a few times since we arrived, but I always feel it guiding. Don't you? But then…then I…I guess I'm just not focusing hard enough to see it."

The room grew silent. There were only a handful of students in town, and most were in the room, chatting, goofing around, still waking up. But everything stopped when Chih-ming mentioned the glow still at work within him. Everyone leaned in. Even Nuzrene, who had witnessed the glow within Chih that morning, paused to hear more about it.

"I do," Joanna said, her voice quiet and thoughtful. "It's different around here, though. I Don't feel it burn the way I did back at the compound. It's more like constant, subtle pressure. It's like it just exists, and that's all."

"Not quite the wild lava-like humanoid or Heschel busting open with rays of light," said Ming, only now realizing the room had shifted all attention his way. With an awkward chuckle and a deep breath, he smacked his hands together, then gave a shout-out to Nuzrene, "I see you're donning the professor badge again today."

"I am…yes…yes, of course. Our fantastic instructor has been called away once again to help with some fall prep," he replied, caught off guard yet just as quick-witted and joyful as usual. "Chih, I'm looking forward to your insights this session."

Joanna turned on the main screen, found an open seat next to Chih, then settled in with her device, ready for notes. Sessions in town were nothing like they had been on Compound 40. She never dreaded the lectures. She hadn't necessarily dreaded the sessions at C-40, but looking back, there also wasn't excitement to attend either. They taught. She listened. Rinse. Repeat. Then the glow appeared, and something shifted. She knew there was more to it than data downloading.

Now, in town, she looked forward to it. One of only seven students, she had grown to appreciate a style of teaching that seemed to emanate from the glow within. Questions were not only allowed but encouraged. Discussion was intentional, challenging, and open to all. And there were stories. Not just groomed narratives, manicured theories, and approved phrases. These stories carried a meaning deep within them, something that had to be contemplated, worked through, and mined for the more profound hidden treasure—the sort of learning she discovered alongside Heschel through the mysterious tablet pieces.

"What would you say if I were to tell you that each of you will either become a mighty tree or a withered bush?"

Nuzrene asked, diving right into the lesson.

Sitting in a semicircle around him, the students looked at one another with uncomfortable smiles. The screen in the background displayed the image of a healthy oak tree rising high above a pitifully malnourished blueberry bush.

"More specifically—a bush in the wastelands or a tree planted by a river."

One by one, the students chimed in. When they answered with a statement, Nuzrene would follow up with another question, only more challenging. If they answered with a question, he would pause, stare through the window at the back of the small room, then respond with as few words as possible and often with another question.

"I wonder if there's more to it than the type of plant," blurted Chih, rudely interrupting another student's verbal processing.

"Go on," said Nuzrene, prone to letting the wild wind of conversation blow where it wanted.

"Sorry…I was just thinking about my time down by the river," said Chih, picturing the vibrant array of flora and fauna teeming along the edge. "Even the smallest plant, including blueberry bushes and oaks, tulips and maples, they're all healthy, and they're all wildly different in size and shape and fruitfulness."

"Like the giant oak in the courtyard at C-40 just a few feet away from the luscious ferns," Joanna joined in.

"Maybe it's more about the environment they're in than the make-up of the plant?"

"I think you're on to something here, you two," said Nuzrene, leaning forward on the stool with a serious look of curiosity. "What is it about the environment?"

"If I'm a blueberry bush, well, no doubt I want to be planted near the water, the nutrients, the source of life," said Chih. "All the more if I'm an oak since I suppose I'd need a little more water to survive."

"So it is about the type of plant, then," Joanna chimed in. "I mean, sure, both the oak tree and the blueberry bush are needed, one for its shade and strong wood, the other for the fruit it provides. And both for survival…but the bigger you are, the more resources you need to stay healthy."

"Okay…so what does this have to do with the glow?" Nuzrene prodded. To him, everything always circled back to this mysterious, ancient, divine power connecting towns and tribes beyond The Chamber's reach worldwide.

"The glow…the glow…well…if I'm an oak in this little story," said Chih, straightening up in his chair, "then maybe it means I have talents, skills, knowledge… hmm…something to offer that's massively beneficial to the community on a large scale. So I'd need to rely on the power of the glow constantly as if it were a flowing river endlessly pumping wisdom and strength and truth into my roots…into my gut."

Nuzrene looked Chih in the eye and gave a subtle nod. Whatever Chih was wrestling with, he knew something in this analogy was ripe for grasping.

"Is that a clue?" Joanna said, her tone shifting from playful and curious to almost accusatory.

"A clue?" asked Nuzrene, still acting in his role as the teacher.

"A clue. A clue! You know, something that's going to get us closer to Hesch. The oak tree, the glow, the power, and the resources?" she stammered. "Obviously, they all point directly to the one person we've been waiting on the elders to rescue since we got here!"

Chih put his hand on Joanna's shoulder. Nuzrene took a deep breath, closed his eyes, and nodded. "I don't blame you for seeing your friend within every analogy. In fact, I'm convinced more and more that the glow is trying to tell you something…tell us all something. But it's not time yet."

"When?" she pressed, her voice shaky and her hands beginning to tremble. "Here I go again. Crying! At least once a week. Why don't you guys do this?"

"And to think The Chamber actually found a way to wash our minds free from even noticing these natural chemical differences," said Chih, squeezing Joanna's shoulder as the group chuckled.

"To be fair, that regulation bubble-dome hairstyle totally

fooled me," said Nuzrene, soft and sarcastic.

The students burst out laughing while Joanna wiped her eyes, laugh-crying and snorting uncontrollably. Because Nuzrene said it, it was all the more amusing. And because she knew he was right. Not about the haircut but about waiting for the right time. Of course the elders knew best.

3 False Alarm

Nuzrene had shut everything in the room down and locked the main door when he felt his device begin to vibrate. Still thinking about Joanna's comments, he didn't immediately acknowledge it. Turning to leave, with a gaggle of oblivious students loitering behind him, he noticed lights flashing through the windows across the narrow street.

"Perimeter breach," he whispered, rubbing his chin and looking up and down the street.

"Another one?" asked Chih, pointing to his device. "Three times in less than two weeks. Is this normal?"

"I don't know any more than you do," he continued

to whisper, cautiously corralling the students toward the maintenance workshop half a block down the street. "Hurry. Stay quiet. You know where to go."

The whole town immediately quashed all noise. After the first false alarm, the students were reminded about the simple process of sheltering, something they had all covered during orientation. Sheltering was simple—follow the leader to safety, then shelter in place until the threat was neutralized. For Chih-ming and Joanna, it wasn't so different than their previous training back at Compound 40: move quickly, stay quiet, follow orders.

The workshop was empty. Benches, machines, and cabinets filled the room. A single light strobed once every second, like a flash of lightning, only controlled.

"Looks like the crew left in a hurry," said Joanna, picking up a rubber mallet left on top of a roll of sheet metal stretched out across a table. "So, do you think this room is bomb-proof or something? Why would we come *here* when everyone else was willing to ditch this place?"

"Chih, give me a hand, will you?" Nuzrene quickly grabbed the end of a table at the center of the room. Chih followed suit. Together, they lifted one end upward. The table legs at the opposite end were secured to the floor like a fulcrum, with a steel cable running through the center of each leg. As they lifted, a weight shifted beneath the floor, sliding open the hidden door and revealing a narrow set of stairs beneath the old wooden floor.

"I know, Chih. Let me stop you before you utter it again. With so many bugs in our tech, the elders decided it best to create something simple and reliable. Something that couldn't be shut down from the outside. After all, it's gotta be difficult to hack into a wooden table." Nuzrene remained calm, not once raising his voice or rushing them along. Like a commentator, he would describe next steps and simple projects in detail. He felt it kept their hearts and minds focused in a crisis. It was evident to the other students that, while he was still a student alongside them, he carried the natural weight of being the oldest, with international experience and a humble brand of confidence.

Several students had already entered the shaft when Joanna paused. "I can't stay quiet. Why do we keep running from the fight? We were trained to obey, sure, but not run and hide. You know this, Nuzrene. No doubt your compound taught the same. Everyone pulls their weight in defense, right?"

Nuzrene stopped. He always paused when confronted with an idea, question, or challenge. Even as the alarm flashed around him, with untold dangers creeping in, he thoughtfully considered her objection. "You're right. I suppose I haven't thought about those days in a while. But we're not on a compound. We're not being trained to be activist-warrior-cogs in some socio-polito-alphabet machine. We're students. We're tasked with carrying the torch for the next generation. And when they need us to step up, we will."

Joanna nodded. She wasn't picking a fight or trying to launch a mutiny. She was a product of compound life, and she had been through a lot over the past year, and now she was curious. She had begun to descend the steps when she noticed the soft, orange glow emanating from Nuzrene's chest and right through his gray t-shirt.

"It's time to go, J. We can dig into student protocol later," said Chih, standing behind her on the top step, still holding a leg of the table.

"Look, Ming. Look at him."

The glow was bright. Not bright enough to wash out the flashing emergency light in the room but enough to stop them in their tracks.

"Remember when I said I haven't really seen the orb in action since we arrived?" mumbled Chih, staring at the glow. "Well… it's not free-floating…but I'd say that's pretty legit."

"Why are you two looking at me like that?" said Nuzrene, patiently holding the table, watching their faces contort in wonder and fear. "Listen, I don't want to…."

"The glow, Nuzrene. It's the glow, and it's, like, really trying to get our attention," whispered Joanna.

Nuzrene looked past Joanna to catch his reflection in a cabinet door along the wall. Without saying a word and keeping his eyes on the orange light, he began patting his chest and arms as if in disbelief that it was his own body he was seeing.

"Are you alright? Does it burn? It always seemed to burn, not like a fire, but like a minty muscle rub, when it would suddenly appear." Chih waved his hand in front of Nuzrene's face. "Hello? Are you in there?"

As if suddenly waking from a terrifying dream, Nuzrene jolted. His eyes were wide as he glanced around. Though he remained calm, beads of sweat were forming on his forehead. As fast as it appeared, the light was gone. They were standing there, looking at one another with a sense of wonder at the strangeness of it all, when the main garage door started to rise.

"Hey, Nuzrene!" called a man from out on the street. "You in there?"

"McCoy? Is everything alright?" Nuzrene replied after a moment of silence, only now realizing the flashing lights had ceased. "We're just working our way into the shelter."

"Now? What's taken so long? I suppose we'd better pick back up on our emergency training by the looks of things." McCoy was a big man, tall, with a broad chest and strong hands. His skin was dark, like Heschel's, and he carried himself the way an honest leader does, with a warmth that invited you not simply to follow, but join him. "Yep, false alarm as far as we can tell."

"Sensors are corroded," Nuzrene said, matter of fact. "I

noticed signs of weathering on my last systems review in the forest."

"Yep, I believe you mentioned that last time. Either that or big ole black bears. Any luck hunting some down on the web? Other towns? Warehouses?"

"Bears?" said Nuzrene, immediately embarrassed.

McCoy made his way to Nuzrene and threw his arm across his young assistant's shoulders. "Sensors," he said with a smile. And with a voice that put them all at ease, he called the students to return to the land of the living and carry on with their schedules.

"You don't think it could be Chicanery and his minions, do you, McCoy?" asked Joanna. "Maybe it's my imagination, but I've seen movement in the woods when I'm alone on the street and outside my window just before lights out. Shadows that move quick."

"Anything's possible," replied McCoy with a deep breath, looking out towards the forest. "Let's keep an eye out around town—all of us. But don't let a fear of the unknown keep you from living your life. Caution, not fear. You're *not* alone."

Making their way up from the pit, each student fist-bumped McCoy before heading outside. Joanna, wanting to say more about the glow, and the false alarm, and rescuing Heschel, looked at Nuzrene and, with a sly smile, simply accepted his earlier words of wisdom. *Be patient,* she told herself.

 # 4 Mystery Maintenance

It was another muggy morning. The river was calm, and the town quiet. Having already spent an hour struggling to translate a few more words, Chih was contemplating what he'd found. For a second, he thought he'd heard a low and guttural growl in the distance. It didn't seem right to ignore it, but it wasn't anything to alert the elders about either.

Most people think of animals when they hear a growl— wild animals like bears, and lions, and feral chipmunks with gnarled ears and unkempt fur. Chih thought of Principal Chicanery.

Shaking the image from his mind, he tried to refocus, but it was too late. The strange growling came and went. But so did a mental replay of Chicanery on stage in Chagrin Center, fuming, knife-wielding, and smiling his creepy, sardonic smile.

What's this all about? I don't know what you're trying to show me? he said, eyes closed and channeling the glow. *Is it connected to the text? Nuzrene?* Chih squirmed a bit, shifting his butt on the hard stone he was perched on. *'In my name...'* he recited. *What name? The name hasn't been found. It's been erased. It's nowhere. 'Ask anything in my name...'* he continued. *Anything? What about Hesch? I didn't mean to leave him. And what about Chicanery and all the power, and evil, and corruption he's perpetrated on the people of the light? On us, students! What am I supposed to ask right now?*

Suddenly, as if sneaking up on him after a slow and steady climb, the growling rose in volume and pitch. It wasn't just louder but more shrill like a wild cat pushed to its limits or the whining whir of a motor.

A motor? It's a boat. Sounds like a small boat.

He had just made the connection when it appeared. Downriver, around the bend, a small aluminum craft forced its way through a brief patch of rapids. The front end popped up over and over, making it difficult to see who was at the helm.

While the mysterious growl had initially made him uncomfortable, the sight of the unknown, unmarked boat did not. Cautious? Of course. But trading wasn't uncommon, and the river was the most likely route.

From a distance, with dawn just breaking and a haze over the river, Chih saw what appeared to be a small light on the backend of the craft near the motor, distinct from the port side light. It rose and fell with the skipper and was hardly bright enough to be worth anything at all on the water.

As the boat drew near, Chih switched on his device, ready to call for help should the mystery turn sour. Coming up fast, the skipper made a wide turn with the craft, dug in deep, then launched itself toward the dirt ramp only a few feet away from the curious student.

"WHOA! What are you doing? You're gonna chew up the propeller. Or worse, get someone killed!" Chih jumped to his feet like a startled dog, barking at the captain while foolishly stumbling backward into a raspberry patch.

With the boat fully on shore and clear of the river, the motor whined to a stop just as Chih began to groan. "Help! I'm stuck. My shirt…and my pants…and skin… Everything's snagged, no thanks to you!"

"Stop tugging and kicking, would ya," came the stern voice of a woman clearly annoyed by Chih's presence. "It's like quicksand. The more you move, the worse it gets."

"What? Who are you? Ouch! Owee! Sheesh!"

"What are you, five? Stop wiggling already," she quipped. Pulling out a wooden-handled machete, she proceeded to hack at the prickly limbs nearest the young man, careful not to kill off more than was needed.

"That was some entrance," muttered Chih, kneeling in the dirt and pulling thorns from his neck and arms. "Is anyone here expecting you?"

Tossing a green backpack to the ground beside the boat, she noticed Chih's little red book face up and opened wide. Next to it was a broken ceramic mug lying in the mud. Looking him up and down, the eccentric woman stepped back and secured her craft.

"Let's go," she said, grabbing her pack and nodding toward the forest.

"Go where? I don't know you. You almost killed me. Why would I trust you? What I ought to do is…."

"Is that really what the glow is telling you about me right now?" she said, with a sharp look at the young man still kneeling in the dirt before turning toward the woods.

Without another word, Chih rose to his feet, dusted himself off, stuffed the red book into his back pocket, and quickly chased after the mysterious invader. Dressed in thick and worn clothing, she looked as though she were ready for an endless winter. She was short and stout. The tough sort of stout that you knew you ought not mess with. She was pretty too. Aside from Joanna, Chih had never thought about someone looking pretty. Words like pretty and handsome had become obsolete, if not entirely banned. After all, the Anti-Libertas worked hard to make their students look and act alike, which only kind of worked. Reality is hard to suppress for too long.

"Your clothes look just like the clothes of someone I saw at the compound this past spring before I got here," he said, talking to break the silence.

She paused for a brief moment. So quick that Chih couldn't be sure, but he felt something when she did. Compassion. Fear. He didn't know what to make of it— so he didn't.

Coming across a small metal stake in the ground, she dropped her pack, then crouched beside it.

"Toss me a Phillips head screwdriver," she said, holding her arm out impatiently. "You do know what a Phillips head screwdriver is, don't you? It's not the flat one, or the star shape, or the square…."

"It's the cross one," he said, placing the handle in her palm. "I'm not five."

"Humph."

For an hour or so, as the sun picked up its pace, the two of them worked their way around the outskirts of the town. Every once in a while, they'd stop, drop the bag, and repeat some of the words and actions of that first repair. Only each time she asked for a different screwdriver, tool, sensor, or sealant. And each time, he felt like a defensive child.

"Seems this is the last one," said Chih, reaching into the bag for a pair of needle-nose pliers. "I probably ought to get back. Nuzrene's gonna be wondering why I'm skipping the morning...."

"Shhh!" she growled, slapping her hand not-so-gently over his mouth. "Bear."

"A meaw? I non't phee a meaw," mumbled Chih, his heart pounding as he crouched lower and lower.

"Hush, child!" she whispered. "Looks like that mountain lion has his eyes set on her."

 **5 Prophetic Delivery**

"**M**unten wion!" muttered Chih, losing his balance in fear. Falling backward onto his butt, his mouth came unmuzzled. "Nuzrene never said anything about lions around here!"

"Are you trying to make us the meal?" she said with a glare more potent than a shock dart. "Ya know, I heard you miraculously escaped Chicanery's rage through the power of the glow. Hmm. From where I stand, you're just a little boy figuring things out. Though I don't doubt it was miraculous."

Chih-ming's eyes narrowed from the wide gaze of panic to focused observation. He had already been feeling low, but now, to have such a bold stranger point out the painfully obvious, his heart sank. Right there in the thick grass, among the wild, overgrown ferns and firebushes, his mind raced through random moments of impact throughout his life.

He saw himself as a child cowering at the center of a crowd in a town square only vaguely familiar. He saw the same boy, scared and shaking, in a familiar flat on Compound 40. Images flashed as he grew up, always hunched over to appear smaller, weaker, unimpressive. His stomach turned as he watched his life as a student lived with his face toward the ground.

Suddenly, he saw himself lying on the floor of the balcony within Chagrin Center as the glow lit up the space around him. He could hear a familiar voice call out, "Stand up. It's time. You were set apart for this, to rise up against the mob with a power greater than we could ever imagine. If we don't stand now, our hearts and minds will crawl on forever."

"Hesch pushed me forward," whispered Chih. "And Joanna stood by my side. But it was the glow that challenged me to live my namesake—to stand with purpose. She's right. It was a miracle. I have no business being here. But…I don't really want to be eaten alive… at least not yet."

He watched as a subtle smile cracked across the woman's face with a faint glow encompassing her.

Pointing up toward the treetops, she paused, her smile growing as the sound of caws and cackles began to fill the air.

"Crows are survivors. They hunt, protect, and are not too proud to scavenge," she said, adjusting her coat.

Listening intently, Chih moved like a sloth, planting his feet firmly, careful to grab hold of sturdy limbs to pull himself upright. He didn't make a sound.

"Pumas are territorial," she continued. "But this black bear, she isn't here to claim ownership of anything other than her need to feed, to care for her young, to weather a storm. She circles the valley, eating and moving, eating and moving. Fish in the river on a good day. Berries, honey, insects…lots of bugs."

"We never really talked about the species in this zone," Chih reflected, whispering as he watched the giant cat slither down the trunk of the tree. "Only that, when they used to live here, past generations of humans killed and scared them off for sport."

"For sport, eh?" The old Deplorable smiled, thinking, *and what was their option, those people, my people, in past generations? To pretend to live harmoniously with killer cats and ferocious mama bears? As if a starving lion wants harmony. To abandon our children to the wilds like human sacrifices?* "Well, it was a bit more than just for sport."

Like McCoy, there was a wisdom, an experiential knowledge that welled up from deep within her. A glowing guidance of life and purpose. "We're designed to be stewards of the world's creatures, Chih. In a perfect universe, sure, our relationship with the great cats might have looked different. But in the real world, like crows, we survive. We hunt when necessary. We protect as well. We even scavenge…Now watch."

She had never experienced life on a compound, but, nevertheless, she had been exposed to the early educational rants of the Alphabet Coup as a young student in her little town. She was well aware of the ironic anti-human language proclaimed by the very same tyrants that demanded communal support and subjugation. They needed humans—only the *right* sort of humans—the ones who followed their progress like sheep. Chih was not a sheep. She had heard the glow was at work within this young man, that Nuzrene saw a bright future ahead for him. She also sensed the tension inside of him and knew the glow still had some serious enlightening to do.

The bear was oblivious. Sitting with its back to the creeping cat, it innocently fed on fresh honeycomb, lost in a world of sweet pleasure. It was the town's honeycomb…or used to be. The students were in charge of tending to it, though, no doubt they'd have to start fresh with a new queen.

"See this?" she whispered, shaking her head. "Distracted by her temporary satisfaction, she's ignoring the threat lurking in the shadows. A threat she's no doubt battled before if those scars on her back have anything to say about it."

Chih remained perfectly still. Altering his attention between the crows above and the action below, he was lost, like the bear, in the moment.

"Take note. The cat doesn't care about fair fights and equitable land management. It's territorial. Nothing more. It wants what it wants and doesn't care what it has to destroy to keep it to itself…himself."

Just then, the puma sprang into action with such a loud screech that Chih fell back in shock once again, only this time quickly scrambling back to his feet, ready to run from the brawl breaking out. Mama bear rolled forward, completely caught off guard with honeycomb now smashed across her face. With bees swarming and honey covering her eyes, she swung her giant paws blindly through the air. The big cat leaped, pounced, clawed, and tore at her flesh. One bite at a time, he lunged until finally, with a roar that echoed through the forest, the bear collapsed.

With a sudden burst of energy, the bear hugged the dangerous feline standing over her, rolled onto its stomach, and smashed the cat between her great weight and the forest floor. The cat screamed and writhed, gasping for air, and with a final explosion of power, sunk its sharp teeth into the neck of the bear. With a violent heave, the two separated.

"Do you hear that?" asked the Deplorable. "Do you hear the crows growing louder? Crows are territorial too. They know full well the cat would eat them without hesitation. And they're sharp. Some of the smartest birds alive. They know when to strike and when to rest…Keep watching."

Without warning, dozens, if not hundreds, of black birds swooped beneath the treetops. As quick as the wind, they encircled the great cat lying wounded and still. They circled several times and then, with a sound that Chih would never forget, descended upon the golden beast in a black cloud of death, pecking, cawing, tearing, and clawing. The cat howled as tufts of fur floated into the air, past the humans, and throughout the forest.

"Chih," said the woman, her voice gentle but gruff. "There are times when a murder of crows can do more for the good of the forest than a giant, powerful, intimidating bear. Sometimes the bear gets comfortable. Sometimes it gets distracted. And sometimes, it takes a tribe of crows, even orphaned ones, to discern the best time to claim the best treasure. Even then, it's a bumpy ride with an endless world of what-ifs. Crows? They decided. Act. Learn and then move on."

Chih grabbed his chest as she spoke. The burn of

the glow began to churn within his heart. He couldn't believe what he had just witnessed. It wasn't that he was offended, after all, something about it seemed wild and natural. It's that it was new and dramatic and full of raw wisdom. He felt the ferocity and the cleverness of the crows. He felt the pain of the bear. He even felt the loss of the cat. But mostly, he felt the rise of the glow within him—sudden and relentless.

"Lions, and bears, and crows like orphans?" he repeated under his breath. "What a morning."

Collecting her tools, the disheveled Deplorable packed her bag, cinched it tight, threw it over her shoulder, then disappeared into the forest back to her boat. Quickly hidden in the thicket and fog, she left just as mysteriously as she had arrived. From the corner of his eye, between the trees and the overgrown ferns, Chih caught sight of what could only be the orb. Zigging and zagging, it glowed steadily even as the boat's motor broke the silence. As the sound faded downriver, so did the glow.

"Joanna's right…the crows have some work to do."

6 Solitary

"Heschel, Heschel, Heschel…Haha! I remember when you first arrived here," snickered Chicanery, sitting on a short metal stool beside the curled-up student inside the hot spot. "I admit it. I sensed something about you from the start. Something The Chamber might have been proud of…had things, you know, turned out differently."

Heschel didn't move a muscle. He didn't make a sound. The young prisoner had grown used to these early morning visits by the unhinged leader of the deranged Anti-Libertas movement. He just sat there with his head in his arms, exhausted, nearly starved, dehydrated, and weak. The sort of weak you feel after running a hundred-yard dash full-on without warming up. Over and over again.

But the young WAFE wasn't just physically weak. Heschel was mentally and emotionally fraying. Monitors were programmed to wake him at random intervals day and night. Never allowed to sleep for more than ninety minutes consecutively, his head pounded, and his muscles twitched. And while the re-education loops failed to brainwash him, they nevertheless exhausted his ability to focus, to think, to allow space for the glow to energize him with clarity and courage. Chicanery knew that a mere sliver of relief was all it would take for the supernatural power of the ancient glow to revive the broken Observer.

"My parents, oops, did I just mention an illicit concept?" Chicanery smiled, elbowing Heschel in the shoulder while laughing a deep-bellied laugh. "I mean, my gestational-host and their life-partner struggled to care for my needs after my birthing process was complete, and so they would send me for long stays with their elders, what we used to call grandparents."

Chicanery drew out the last word as if trying to hold onto it. His red, irritated eyes seemed to glaze over for a moment before snapping back to his story with a snarl.

"They were like your people," he growled, anger churning deep in his throat. Clenching his fists, he forced the story out. "Deplorables...loosely connected to the people of the light. They were simple, hardworking elders with a natural sort of faith in the world. They held onto an unrealistic hope that their farm would survive the Alphabet Coup's terror on independent makers, shapers, farmers, and thinkers. A wasted hope."

Chicanery stopped. He stopped speaking, snickering, and shifting in his seat. Instead, Heschel heard the steady sound of drops hitting the cold, hard tile floor. Then a sniffle. And another.

Drawing enough strength to lift his head, the student watched the most villainous human in the modern era weep over the memory of his grandparents. With his head in his hands, his back heaving, and tears pooling at his feet, Chicanery let it all out—a big, snotty, moany cry that totally consumed him for several minutes.

You don't have to…Heschel began to say from deep within, somehow still capable of communicating with the devious leader through the glow.

"STOP!" Chicanery shouted, forcefully pounding his fists on the padded wall behind him. "I don't need a pep-talk from a deluded child. There's no such thing as hope—only submission and concession. The only traits a child needs to endure the Anti-Libertas way. Traits you've failed to grasp. You're an ignorant creature rotting here because of your foolish hope and failed subordination. 'Hope never disappoints,' they used to say. Well…it does. It *always* does."

On the heels of his final word, a green LED on the ceiling began to flash, washing over everything in the tiny room. Heschel, staring at the floor, took note and waited for the door to open. Chicanery's visits were random, often volatile, and without any sort of timeframe.

"Master Chicanery," said the highly decorated monitor, "I see you're still working directly with the virus." His voice was familiar. One Heschel hadn't heard since the day he was thrown into the hot spot.

"The evil twin," said Heschel, his first spoken words in nearly two months.

Chicanery flashed his wide, red eyes toward the sickly student. Holding his stare, he cut straight to the point with the deputized monitor standing by.

"Keep it short."

"Seems the bear is still asleep," said the monitor, speaking in code. "We've poked the den from all sides and each time without pushback. Sources tell me McCoy believes it's nothing more than wild animals and corroded sensors. Fools. However...."

Chicanery's eyes shifted back and forth, waiting for the bad news. "However, what?"

"It's...It's nothing," he mumbled half-heartedly.

"If you're unable to lead the hunt, I'll...."

"It's not that..." he stammered, eyes boring into Chicanery. "I felt something in those woods. You, of all people, know what I mean. The sort of pull that always seems to emanate from that supernatural orb. I've felt it around the entire perimeter these last few months."

"So it's confirmed then," whispered Chicanery. "Our missing pupils really are being sheltered downriver."

"I suppose you're right," he replied, breathing deeply with a wide smile. "I hadn't connected the two." The unsettling memory of the orb's power melted away as quickly as it had risen. After the chaos in the museum, Chicanery ordered all monitors to be re-educated—all but one.

As the leader of The Chamber, he wanted a clear-minded partner to witness the chaotic abuse the glow heaped on Compound 40. And the evil twin, whose deplorable brother remained locked in the hot spot down the hall, was the perfect Anti-Libertas lackey for the job. Experienced. Obedient. However, not as confident as Chicanery in their ability to detain the glow.

"So the lion is still ready to strike?" asked the principal, rising to his feet. His red eyes stared down the monitor like a cat sizing up a mouse.

"Very soon, Principal Chicanery. We're preparing now," replied the monitor, nervous and giddy like a child waiting to open a present.

Chicanery nodded as the evil twin turned, pulled some forest debrief from his uniform, then smiled, holding it up for Heschel to see. "I'm told your friends have settled in well. So well, in fact, that they no longer think of you. Seems you've been completely forgotten in their escape, huh?"

Isn't that what you trained them to do, Chicanery? said Heschel, his lips remaining still while his mind worked overtime to communicate. *Progress before people, right?*

You've managed to hold onto your sarcasm. How mature! replied Chicanery, mind to mind. *So much for that tight-knit murder of crows. I guess three's a crowd. But don't worry...I'll be personally checking in on them soon enough. I think I'm going to enjoy this little hunting expedition.*

7 Just a Dream

She was covered in sweat. Her pulse was racing. Alma and Adia, the two other girls sharing a room with her, were standing on either side of Joanna's bed, trying to wake her. Again.

"Open the windows, would you, Alma? Maybe the morning air will help calm her down."

This wasn't the first time nightmares wrecked a good night's sleep. The girls' new roommate from Compound 40 was incredibly kind, sharp, and brave, but she also required a bit of care. They knew she had been through a lot, though Joanna didn't share much. And while they were eager to learn about the glow, thankful to be among so many extraordinary people, they hadn't actually experienced the power of the orb for themselves.

This morning was different though. This wasn't the typical nightmare at work.

"Adia, we need Maria," said Alma, her voice shaking along with her hands. "She'll know what to do. Something's different this time."

Alma wasn't gone long. Maria was in her home only a block away. Dressed and ready for the day before sunrise, she dropped the clothes she had been mending and rushed to the girls' dorm house.

"How long has she been twisting and turning like this?" asked Maria, wiping the sweat from Joanna's forehead with one of the girls' towels.

"We don't really know," said Adia. "We both woke up to her talking in her sleep just before the morning alarm went off. She was dripping with sweat, her cheeks were red, and her blanket was piled on the floor."

Maria placed a hand on Joanna's shoulder, closed her eyes, bowed her head, then took several deep, slow breaths. After nearly fifteen minutes Joanna calmed down. At the same time, the girls thought they saw a faint light emanate from between Maria's palm and Joanna's forehead. Not so much a direct light but the reddish glow of skin over a lightbulb.

"It's not a nightmare... It's a vision...I can hear his

voice!" Maria jolted upright, pulled her hand from Joanna's forehead, then calmly but sternly, commanded the girls' attention. "Adia, get some fresh water and a cup with a straw. Alma, gather a pad and pencil. Write down everything I describe to you. Don't ask. Just write."

"Is everything going to be okay? Is she hurt?" asked Alma, her voice still quivering.

Maria, always kind but rarely one to show physical displays of affection, smiled. Alma and Adia were both relieved and startled to see Maria break character like that.

Without wasting time, Maria once again placed her hand on Joanna. This time, however, she simply grabbed hold of her cold, sweaty hand.

Once again, she bowed her head, closed her eyes, breathed deep, then waited. Only this time, she didn't have to wait long.

"There's a brown bear…No! A black bear. I see a black bear sitting peacefully in the forest," she whispered, gruff yet clear. As she spoke, the glow between their palms slowly illuminated more and more. "I recognize the honey box and the trails winding through the trees. The bear is sitting in our forest."

"Is this really happening, Maria?" asked Adia, returning with the water.

"Shhh. I need to listen. I need you to be silent."

Feeling bad about interrupting, Adia set the water down on the bedstand and began to fade into the background.

"No. Stay. Dab her head with water and let her drink some if she asks. You're doing fine," reassured Maria. The smile was gone, but her voice was gentle as ever.

"I see something else moving in the tree. It's a lion. A mountain lion. It's hunting the bear! Stalking her as she quietly, carefully consumes the honeycomb. The bear doesn't hear a thing. Why doesn't she hear it? Or sense it?"

Maria shook her head, pinching her eyes so tight that her wrinkled nose and cheeks turned bright red. Glued to the frightening display before them, the girls watched as rays of light darted out from between clasped hands as the mysterious transmission unfolded. Scooting closer and closer together, the girls huddled up beside the bed, courageously scribbling notes and caring for their new friend.

"NO! The bear...attacked...now fighting, clawing, scraping...and biting," Maria cried out in bursts. Her voice wobbled more and more as the scene unfolded. "She's terribly hurt," she whispered, dropping her shoulders and lowering her head. "But so is the lion. The lion is...the lion... it's killed the bear. Now they're both just lying on the forest floor, still as death."

For a while, Maria didn't say a word. She just sat

there holding Joanna's hand. Her face relaxed though still concerned. The girls sat in silence, waiting for their trusted leader to make the next move.

"The glow…I see it," she finally added, lifting her head as if she could see it in real-time. "There, up in the sky, just above the treeline, safely watching the attack from above. There's a voice…and it's coming from the glowing orb. Heschel's voice? No…not Hesch…but familiar…A warning!"

All of a sudden Joanna sat up in bed. Her eyes, like headlights, glared at Maria.

"The lion's losing his grip, and the bear's slumbering. It's time for her to wake up. The crows need to fly. Where's Chih?" As quick as she sat up, Joanna fell back onto her pillow, passed out cold. The glow was gone.

"Girls," said Maria, "I need McCoy. As quickly as you can. And find Chih. Check the boat ramp."

 **8 Connect the Dots**

Maria was sitting on the front porch, watching the fog roll up from the river. The town was old, 1800's old. Years before McCoy arrived it had been deserted, left to the wilds. Too close to Compound 40.

But that's precisely why McCoy chose it. He was clear-minded and strong-willed. The glow had given him a vision of the future collapse of the Anti-Libertas, and he wanted to be as close as possible when it happened.

Waiting for the girls to return with Chih and McCoy, Maria couldn't help but think about Charlie. Just hearing Heschel's voice triggered memories of the entire ordeal on the edge nearly a year ago. Her anger at The Chamber.

The simmering bitterness she had felt toward everyone around her. The rage she gave into when she discovered that students found the clues she had given up on years before.

Charlie's death is my fault. I can't change that. I'll never be able to make that right, she thought, wringing her cold hands together. It was the same oppressive internal story she had told herself from the moment she was rescued on the river. Not a day passed when she didn't consider the mortal weight of her actions.

And now, through Joanna's vision, the reality of pulling Charlie from the rocks with a belligerent disregard for life—hers and his—was so visceral she could smell the waterfall, feel her scratched-up and bleeding hands, and see the horrifying look on Heschel's face when Charlie finally let go.

Sitting on the front porch, Maria was lost in self-pity when Joanna stepped outside to stretch her legs, unaware of the prophetic rollercoaster she'd taken them on.

"Maria?" Joanna whispered, the cold air striking her sweaty arms and face, causing her to cinch the blanket over her shoulders a little tighter.

"You shouldn't be up," said Maria, staring into the fog. "I sent the girls for help."

"Maria, are you alright? I think I remember my dream this time. I never remember them. Why did you send for help? Are you okay?"

Half-dazed from the traumatic memory, Maria locked eyes with Joanna. "Talk to Chih. You said you needed to talk to him. The girls didn't find him but you know where he likes to perch in the mornings. Don't miss a chance to do right."

Looking up and down the street at the fog swirling about, Joanna took off toward the river.

"Ming? Ming! We need to talk!" she cried out as she felt the slope of the boat ramp. Though merely ten feet away from the stone Chih used as a bench, she couldn't see anything through the fog. Checking her device for the umpteenth time, she sat on the cold rock, legs shaking and mind racing. *Where else could he be?*

"What are you doing here?" asked Chih, his voice emerging from the woods. It had been fifteen minutes since she arrived, and was quietly watching fish in the eddy beneath her feet.

"There you are, you two!" said McCoy trying to catch his breath. "I just spoke with Maria. Is it true?"

"Is what true?" asked Chih impatiently.

"You mean Joanna hasn't told you about the vision?" said the elder, finding a clean stone along the riverbank. Perching next to Joanna, he took several depth breaths. "Chih, come have a seat."

"Vision? How did you hear what that mysterious

woman said this morning?" asked Chih, scratching his head as he sat beside them.

"Mystery woman?" said McCoy, his voice loud and high-pitched. "Oh, oh, oh…okay. You met Mrs. Sibyl, did you? So she finally got around to testing the sensors. Intense woman. In tune woman."

"Mrs. Sibyl? Ming, what were you doing with an intense woman in the woods? Where were you just now?" Joanna leaned back, crossed her arms, then stared her friend down like a mama bear would a predator.

"Alright…alright… let's take a breath and start from the beginning," interrupted McCoy. "Joanna, I need to know more about your vision. I've read the transcript. I've heard what the girls had to say. But I need to hear it from you. And so does Chih."

"L…L…Lion?" choked Chih. "So you *were* following me?"

McCoy held up his hand, halting Chih from going any further. "Go on, Joanna. What do you remember?"

"All of it. The entire fight. The bloody death. The orb in the sky leading a murder of crows," she whispered, looking back and forth between the two of them. "And a familiar voice at the end. A warning, I guess, that the crows are fighting and the lion is weakening. I can't put a face to the voice—just that it's tired and urgent. Maria thought it was Heschel, but I don't know. Is that strange?"

"You said the bear needs to wake up…that the crows need to fly." McCoy looked over the notes the girls had taken, soaking in what he believed was the only possible meaning.

"I think we're the bear," she said. "Well, you are, anyhow. And the town. The Deplorables and the people of the light, I guess."

"Bear?" gruffed Chih.

"I think you're right about that," McCoy humbly agreed, his gentle voice trailing off in thought.

"That's what I was up to this morning with the mystery…I mean, with Mrs. Sibyl," said Chih.

"What do you mean?" Joanna asked, clearly confused.

"The bear and the lion. I saw them."

"Well, yeah, if we're the bear, then that makes sense," said McCoy, "but are you saying that you saw *Chicanery* in the woods this morning?"

"If you're saying that Chicanery is now a lion, then yeah, I saw Chicanery…I mean a lion," exclaimed Chih, still scratching his head and shrugging his shoulders. "Look, I actually saw a lion attack a bear in the forest this morning. It was crazy! The bear was eating honey when the lion crept up and bombarded her. Then, out of nowhere, hundreds of crows swooped down and pecked the lion to death."

"What did Mrs. Sibyl do?" asked McCoy.

"She was a rock. Didn't even flinch. Me? I shook like an orphaned fern caught in a hurricane! It was terrifying." His voice grew louder and louder as he spoke. "She said that too. Not the fern part, but she said orphan, which really unsettled me. She narrated the entire fight, basically saying everything you two just said. It's strange too, and I can't explain it, but slowly the fear I had when the animals first started fighting, it turned to purpose. It was like our mission became more and more obvious as the battle raged."

"You're saying the crows didn't just watch from above but descended on the wounded lion?" asked Joanna. "Did you see the orb?"

"The only glow came from Mrs. Sibyl. It wasn't obvious the whole time, but it was there," he said. "You're right, McCoy. She's in tune if anyone is."

"Heschel's okay. He's alive, anyhow. I feel it. And even if he sounds different, he's finally able to communicate," said Joanna, trying to bring all this talk of animals and battles back to the only thing that mattered to her, freeing Heschel from Compound 40. "It's gotta be him, but why do you think he's reaching out now? What took so long? What do we do about it?"

Chih took a deep breath. "He's desperate. It must be getting pretty dangerous up there. Don't you think? I shouldn't have left him."

"I think it's time the bear wakes up," said McCoy, sketching some notes on a blank page in the journal. "The lion's planning something, and it's time we took him seriously. And from what I can tell, the glow is leading the way at the helm of a murder. If it were just a dream, I'd cautiously wait. But it's more than that. The vision, the actual attack in the woods, Mrs. Sibyl confirming it all, the voice calling out for help. I can't deny it."

Joanna, caught off guard, having assumed McCoy would tell them they needed to be patient and wait for the bear to make the first move, tossed the blanket from her shoulders.

"Are you saying what I think you're saying?" she said, her wide eyes bearing down on the elder.

"You two know the grounds better than anyone," McCoy began, continuing the write. "You have an unbreakable connection with Heschel and the glow. But you'll need another crow and a solid plan. Let me talk with the elders and I promise you the wheel will be in motion by this evening."

Joanna was so giddy at the thought of seeing Heschel again that she leaped forward, squeezing McCoy and swaying back and forth. The old man smiled. His daughter used to respond likewise. "Okay. Alright now. That'll do. I know, I know. Alrighty then…."

"I know why *orphan* hit me in the gut. I think I've figured it out," whispered Chih in the midst of Joanna's excitement.

Joanna released her bear hug and joined McCoy in giving attention to Chih.

"'I will not leave you as…uh…hold on…there it is…orphans,'" he began, reading from the little red book. "'I won't leave you as orphans. I will come to you.'" Is this what's happening? We were forced into compound life away from our families. We were forced into orphanhood…and this *father*, this *counselor*, this *glow*…it came for us like it never intended for us to stay orphaned." McCoy and Joanna sat perfectly still, pondering the deep connections Chih was sharing from the text. "I don't know if we'll ever find our families again…but we don't have to be orphans anymore. We have this *spirit*—this *glow*. We have each other. And we have Heschel…who won't be orphaned by us."

Joanna nodded, leaned forward, then wrapped Chih up in a big hug.

"This won't be easy. If Heschel's right, the compound has devolved into something like a wild pride, a new generation of lion cubs coming into their own. Drawing lines. Dividing. You won't know who you can trust…if anyone," McCoy offered, adding to the sobering image expressed by Chih. "Do me a favor. Until we meet again tonight, don't say a word to anyone, alright?"

9 A Normal Day

Nuzrene pulled the stool into the middle of the semicircle. He looked around at the small band of students encircling him.

"Listen, I know the morning has been a little chaotic," Nuzrene said, breaking the abnormal silence in the stuffy little living room turned equipping center. "And that McCoy and the elders have called an emergency meeting…but that doesn't mean we shut down. It doesn't mean we let fear of the unknown sabotage our time together. So until we hear otherwise, answer me this.…"

Nuzrene dove into the lesson like any other morning. Their little world was upending, yet, like Heschel, he seemed to be able to focus on the *right-nows* in place of the *could-bes*.

With a clear mind, he immediately channeled the ancients. Question. Answer. Respond with a question. Answer with a question. Follow up that question with a deeper question. And so on. He was a good teacher. He was really good. It's why McCoy insisted that he join the murder. That he become a crow alongside Chih and Joanna. That, and Nuzrene had also experienced the mind-breaking toll of compound life. And survived.

"So tell me then," the young assistant continued, strolling outside the half circle, "how do you galvanize character within a student?"

"Galvanize?" asked Adia, looking at the question on the screen as though expecting the definition to magically appear.

"Good!" Nuzrene replied with obvious pleasure. "Seeking clarity before attempting an emotional reply. Nice, Adia. Anyone have a definition before jumping on the chain?"

"It's sort of like stirring to action, at least in one sense. On the other hand, it's like solidifying or strengthening something," said Chih, leaning forward in his chair while studying the natural curves of the grain in the hardwood floor.

"They go hand in hand, don't you think?" chimed in

Alma. "Like, when you commit to something, you're solidifying your resolve to get it done. That's both strength and action working together."

Nuzrene stopped in his tracks. Adjusting the collar on his shirt, he made his way back to his stool, revealed the definition on the screen, then put his hands together in a prayer position. Politely bowing toward Alma, he said, "Nicely done bringing those together in real-time, Alma. Very well done, group."

"However?" nudged Joanna, having quickly learned that Nuzrene is never really satisfied.

"However," repeated Nuzrene with a smile, "I didn't hear any follow-up questions in those replies. You shared what you know, or at least what you think you know, yet, you didn't share with us what you don't know…which at your age—my age—is even more important."

The group chuckled at Nuzrene's comment, considering he wasn't much older than them, though he definitely seemed like it at times.

"So, Joanna, how do you galvanize character?" he said, bringing the conversation back on point. "Let's say you're asked to keep a secret. A healthy secret. And by a trusted confidant. Then along comes another friend who that very secret may impact. What would a student of character do?"

Joanna had just taken a sip of hot tea from her mug

when Nuzrene mentioned *secret*. Completely blindsided by the ironic example—McCoy having just asked her to keep their mission a secret—she inhaled her lemon tea and began to choke, spitting water on everyone around her. Considering it's a small group, everyone received a dose of warm, lemon-flavored, Joanna-kissed water.

Choking, and coughing, and snortling, she mumbled words and broken sentences. The group laughed while Chih half-heartedly patted her back and began to wipe up the tea spray covering the floor, chairs, and screen behind Nuzrene. The ho-hum morning had finally felt normal.

"Feels like the chaos has caught up with someone!" said Nuzrene, wiping water from his cheerful face while calmly shutting down the equipment. "Let's call it an early session. Take some time this morning to write out your response to the question. Writing means thinking, and thinking means growing. You're not tree stumps, you're tree trunks. Let's grow!"

The group laughed at another one of Nuzrene's many metaphors. As the students made their way to the door, he took a chance.

What do you say you two crows stick around for a minute? Nuzrene said, directing his thoughts toward Joanna and Chih.

Joanna had just taken another sip of tea when Nuzrene

made the offer. His voice broke her chain of thought. Without making a sound, his voice cut through crisp and clear. Caught off guard again, she spit out her tea as if blowing a raspberry. This time, however, Nuzrene was prepared, jumping back to avoid another shower.

"I thought as much. You know, don't you?" said Chih. It was less of a question and more of a clarifying statement—something to call out the elephant in the room. Or, in this case, the lion, bear, and crows in the room.

"To be honest, I don't really know how I know," Nuzrene said, sounding genuinely mystified. "No doubt it's the glow at work, but that's about all I've had time to consider."

"So McCoy hasn't reached out to you yet?" asked Joanna, wiping the last few drops of tea from her chin. "Was it a vision? Did you hear something in the woods this morning?"

"Nope. Nothing of the sort," he replied, looking around as though he were about to reveal classified information. "It's strange, but it started as a feeling just after sunrise this morning. I was up, following my daily ritual, and then…well… there's really not much to it. I just sensed that you two were being sent away. A mission. A secret. A dangerous one. And that you'd need my help."

"That's it?" said Chih, his voice crackling in a high-pitched crescendo. Clearing his throat several times, with a few false starts at forcing a deep voice, he reiterated, "What I mean to say is, that's all? No glow? No tugging and pulling orb? No secret messages or visions? No creepy voices wafting on the wind?"

"I take it you have a little personal experience with those sorts of interactions with the glow?"

"A little! Are you kidding me? That orb nearly knocked me out cold in their flat," Chih exclaimed, pointing at Joanna. "It's pushed and pulled in so many directions I couldn't tell you what it wanted. It even whispered once! Whispered in - to - my - *ear*. Have you ever had an invisible being whisper directly into your ear? Breathiness and all? Nearly peed myself on that one."

Nuzrene lost it. Bent over laughing, he slowly made his way to the wall for support, gasping for air and waving at Chih to stop. Joanna couldn't help it either. Though none of this had seemed funny at the time, now, at a safe distance, she couldn't help but laugh imagining all of their first experiences with the glowing orb.

"We must have looked...so silly...haha...trying to play it cool around this...this supernatural being.... We were...were absolutely terrified...haha...at its existence!" she muttered in between hackles and crackles.

Chih didn't find it all that funny. He could still feel the

breath of the orb on his ear. It still creeped him out, even in his growing respect for it.

"Listen," Chih continued, "we'll tell you more tonight. McCoy said the elders would decide the next step. We know we're going. And that a murder of crows will be the downfall of Chicanery. And we know we're going soon…."

"We just don't have all the details yet," Joanna added, offering a little support to her fellow crow. "I'm sure McCoy will connect with you soon. He personally wants you to go. Honestly? We need you."

Chih nodded without hesitation. He had already grown to admire Nuzrene and felt better about the mission with him involved.

"I know you've been waiting for this too," Nuzrene said before they left. "I feared you two would make a reckless move and head off to C-40 on your own, without permission…or support. But this? Waiting for the glow to make the first move. To let this mysterious guide change the elders' hearts and minds? That takes a serious level of maturity and, well, faith."

Chih fist-bumped Nuzrene while Joanna reached out for a quick side hug. Like any other day, the two of them headed down the street to wrap up their lesson and find their way to the community kitchen to help prepare lunch. It was an ordinary afternoon.

10 The Hot Spot

The room was darker than midnight without a moon. There were no windows in the hot spot. No light fixtures, switches, or outlets. Even the door cracks were sealed with rubber gaskets to keep the light out and the sound in.

The only external connection was an air vent in the ceiling and a super slim return vent at the base of one of the walls. Neither was large enough to crawl through.

Heschel's eyes had grown used to the dark. At first, his eyes ached from the strain of trying to see. But once he accepted his new reality, he was able to adjust. He still couldn't see anything, of course, but after months in the hole, he began to sense the location and shape of an object.

When Chicanery would visit, or a monitor deliver his food for the day or toiletries for the week, Heschel would simply tuck his face into his folded arms resting on his knees to avoid the glare. Sometimes, for fun, monitors would make their deliveries with an unnecessarily large million candlepower spotlight. They'd flash it all around the little room, taunting him, "Looks like the magic orb is back to save the day!" Then they'd switch it off, "Oops, would you look at that! The little ball of light abandoned you again. Boo-hoo! Poor little boy lost his magical nightlight."

Most of the time, Heschel would patiently ignore the intrusion into his quiet space. But once in a while, it would unnerve him. He'd question if the wild events ever really happened in the first place. If he hadn't just imagined it all. If his friends really did think about him.

They haven't, ya know.

"Who said that?" asked Heschel, startled awake by a voice that bypassed his ears and traveled straight to his mind. His voice was hoarse, and his throat dry.

The one who got you into this crazy mess.

"The Deplorable? I recognize your voice," said Heschel, slowly grasping what was happening. "Strange how our internal voices sound just like our audible ones…And you didn't get me into anything I wasn't already nose-deep in."

I never thought about our voices like that before. I suppose our voice is more entangled with our spirits than we realize.

"Wait…Where are you? Why haven't we connected sooner?"

I'm in the hot spot—same as you, the Deplorable replied. *I didn't know you were here either until this morning.*

"Really? Who told you?"

I felt something. I heard the lion's plan to creep up on the bear and destroy her once and for all. Then I sensed your intensity, eventually hearing your inner voice pleading with your friends.

"I've been trying to connect with Chih and Joanna for months," said Heschel, his voice getting raspy and his throat beginning to ache. "I've tried at all hours of the day, every day. Nothing. But…if you've heard me…I mean, if the glow finally connected you to my, my broadcast…then maybe they heard it too?"

I'm sorry I got you into this. I should never have passed along that memory drive.

"We would have ended up here one way or another," Heschel replied, his eyes beginning to water. It was an emotional thing speaking with another human, another suffering soul, another person of the glow after all this time alone. "None of that matters, though, does it? We're here, and we need to find a way to connect with Chih and Joanna. And we need to do it soon."

I have an idea, said the Deplorable after several minutes of silence.

"Hold on," interrupted Heschel, "I don't even know your name. I've just been calling you the Deplorable, but that's not cool. You risked your life to rescue us. That's not a detestable thing to do. Speaking the truth in the face of The Chamber—*to* their face—knowing that truth is illegal misinformation…propaganda…conspiracy…."

Sibyl. My students call me Mr. Sibyl. My wife calls me crazy. Sorry, old-school dad joke.

"Dad joke? What's that? Is a dad like a father? Like the one from the text? Are all dad jokes like that?" asked Heschel, his voice curiously emboldened.

Yeah. Dads are fathers. And out there, in homes and small towns, they have this unique superpower called the dad joke. But no, most dad jokes aren't as good as that one.

"Are you a dad?" Heschel asked.

No. I'm not, he said softly after a quiet moment. But there's a rule that you naturally earn the right to tell dad jokes at a certain age, regardless.

The conversation paused for a few minutes. Mr.

Sibyl's mind drifted, and his eyes watered at the mention of his wife and the students he taught. Heschel had been motivated months before by Mr. Sibyl's courage during that secret meeting with Chicanery and The Chamber. But now, realizing that he had a life outside of the hot spot, his sacrifice in bringing them the USB was even more honorable in Heschel's mind. They both needed a moment to regroup.

Listen, we've been trying to reach out beyond these walls. We know the glow is at work, but something's not right. Something's keeping us from making a deeper connection. At least, that was until this morning. Something's changed, and I think we need to work together.

"Crows," whispered Heschel, imagining the giant oak in the courtyard covered in large, black birds. And his friends.

In brief, upsetting waves, he'd reflect on friendship, real friendship, and sacrifice, and truth despite suffering. He'd think about the clarity and confidence that emanated from the glow, and the division it brought into his life. And he'd feel alone. Deeply alone in the hot spot, wondering if he wouldn't have been better off a cog in the Anti-Libertas machine. Then the emotional wave would subside and he'd remember that, deep down, even in his most obedient Observer state, he had already felt lonely. He just didn't know what to call it.

I heard an old story about a couple of men of the light, partners in the glow through and through, chained to a wall in a nasty little prison years ago. They had been abused, neglected, mocked, restrained, stripped of their rights, and...well, you get it.

"So what did they do? I assume they escaped, right?" asked Heschel, curious but growing exhausted. "I mean, that's why you're sharing this story."

They sang.

"Hmm...Uh-huh...Did you just say they sang?"

They sang an ancient hymn. A song about this mysterious guide. And it changed the outcome of their confinement. Mr. Sibyl let the story sink in. Though, after hearing it out loud, he wondered if it sounded more absurd than it initially did in his mind.

Listen, Mr. Sibyl, I'm sorry to say this, but I'm too exhausted to understand how singing, an action I've never participated in, could possibly help us. I'm not even sure I could learn how, Heschel replied, pushing through the pounding headache bubbling up. *Whatever you decide...I'm in. I don't get it, sure, but, I trust you.*

Okay then, replied the Deplorable in a reassuring tone. *I'll wake you when it's time.*

11 The Rush

"Dinner smells great!" Chih declared. It was his turn to man the grill, and he loved to baste McCoy's famous barbeque sauce on thick. "Hey, Adia? You know how to tell when it's time to brush on another layer of sauce?"

"No, Chih," she said sarcastically, rolling her eyes.

"Wait, have I told you my secret before?" he said cautiously.

"Only every time you're on duty," she shot back. "And by the way…McCoy does it the same way. In fact, he perfected the crispy edge long before you arrived. So that you know."

Chih blushed, began to shrink back in embarrassment,

but then stopped. Remembering his namesake—one who stands tall with purpose—he took the opportunity to squash his pride and replace it with a new culinary adventure.

"Hey, Adia?" he yelled as she made her way back to the garden to pick a few more peppers. "You know what happens when you baste a Giant Marconi with McCoy's secret sauce?"

Adia stopped. Raised an eyebrow in thought. Then turned back towards Chih, shrugging her shoulders. "Actually, no. I don't. Is it any good?"

Chih smiled, his cheeks still bright red. "I have no idea. How about we find out when you come back with a couple?"

Adia smiled at the idea of creating something fresh. Turning to make her way back to the garden—it happened. The silent alarms were triggered. Strobing lights flashed from the sides of buildings and light posts all around them. Everyone froze.

"Nuzrene, Chih, Joanna—you three head to the river," said McCoy, calm but firm. "The rest of you, head to the bunker."

Without another word, the students dispersed. Once again, their militaristic Anti-Libertas training kicked in, and the three of them diligently headed for the river, only stopping for supplies. Joanna followed Nuzrene to the armory, where three backpacks and a small pile of supplies were prepared and stored for their mission. Chih, however, headed for his room, hoping to grab notes on the text, the little red book, and a few scraps of paper he'd held onto during his escape.

"No, no, no, no, no!" he gruffed under his breath, stopping short of his dorm house before ducking behind an adjacent building. Pulling up his device, he knew he had to warn the others quickly. "They're here! In town! I just saw a handful of monitors enter my dorm…my home. I'm scrapping my plan and will meet you down by the river."

It happened fast. Nuzrene and Joanna showed up just after Chih. They were divvying up the supplies when McCoy arrived.

"In the water…Everyone in the water," McCoy said, corralling the students several feet downriver and behind an outgrowth of trees along the bank. "I'm sorry it has to happen this way. I'd hoped for more—for a greater commissioning. But this will have to do."

Grabbing McCoy's shoulder, Nuzrene reassured him of the plan. "You've done everything you could. You're a great leader and a great model of faith under the knife. This is entirely out of your control, and we all know that."

McCoy's eyes began to water. Nodding in gratefulness,

he didn't waste a moment. "You know the plan. Rescue Heschel. Grab any data you can on Chicanery's abuses. And, if the stars align, locate that hidden entrance behind the falls on your return, the one your friend Charlie discovered. Good?

"Heschel. Data. Entrance. Ditto," echoed Chih, his eyes fastened on McCoy. "I heard someone around here say 'the real McCoy' once. Is that you? Is there a fake? Are you the real McCoy?"

"That was my great, great, great granddaddy, the famous inventor…but I'll tell that story another day," said McCoy, huddling up the students and leaning in close. With their heads touching and their eyes closed, he commissioned them with an ancient benediction he only half-remembered. "May the glow keep you and guide you. May it shine its light on you. May it show you grace and peace."

Quick hugs and fist-bumps all around.

"And Chih, you didn't abandon Heschel," said McCoy. "You need to hear it. And believe it. And bring him back the way you did with Joanna."

Chih's eyes watered as his chest burned. Mouthing *thanks*, he turned away.

Silently the students waded shoulder-deep to the other side of the river, some ten yards across. Hiding in the brush on the other bank, they turned one last time to give a thumbs up to McCoy.

Staring at them with a look of urgency and channeling the glow, he passed along one final note. *Don't worry about us. Work your way to the safe zone, then hunker down until dark. Don't be rash—support each other and don't look back.*

The students looked at one another with sober expressions. The glow was at work more and more, and all three students could feel it stirring.

With a final thumbs up and a reassuring smile, McCoy turned, slogged his way up the boat ramp, and quickly made his way back into town.

 12 Attack! Attack!

No one made it to the bunkers.

The deputized monitor led a well-trained troop quickly and quietly into the heart of the town, tasing, shocking, and rounding everyone up along the way. The screams were few at first. An elder refusing to stand down. Maintenance personnel attempting to get to the armory. Townies pulled from homes and offices. Soon, however, cries for help began to multiply, echoing off the treeline surrounding the town and across the river.

"You two hear that?" asked Joanna, pausing mid-step hardly any distance at all from the river's edge.

"Yeah…I do," said Chih, shaking his head. "We can't

just leave them, Nuzrene. You've known them longer than we have. Those are your people. We can't just ignore it, can we?"

Nuzrene stood still, quietly listening to the sounds. He wasn't one to let emotion take the lead. He nodded, looking both Chih and Joanna in the eyes, then back toward the screams. "We're no good to Heschel or any of the elders if we get caught. They know how to handle themselves—they're trained."

"But…" Joanna blurted out.

"But you're right. We can't just abandon them," Nuzrene followed up. "Let's sit along the river in the brush until we have a better gauge of the chaos. If we can do anything to help, we will. Otherwise, we're just watchmen keeping tabs. Okay?"

It wasn't long before the cries for help, and the growled commands died down. Those who hadn't passed out from the super-charged shock darts were rounded up like cattle, forced to sit in the middle of the road, and encircled by roughly 100 well-armed monitors from rooftop to alleyway, hyped and ready for action.

"Can I help you, gentlemen?" said McCoy, making his way toward the center of town from the river. Lighting a cigar, he offered one to the lead monitor, ignoring the calls by various troops to drop to his knees. "I'm the mayor around here. But of course, you already know that. If you'd like to have a discussion like reasonable adults, let all these fine folks go while you and I chat over coffee. What do you say?"

Without fail, the monitor's kept their rifles pointed at the brave soul, parting them like Moses did the sea. Shoulder's back and head high, McCoy walked toward his people at the center of it all.

"Ahh, McCoy," said the deputized monitor in charge. "Just the Deplorable I wanted to see. Where are they?"

"One-five-zero-one," replied McCoy, reciting the monitor's serial number like an old acquaintance, keeping one eye on him and one eye on his people. "Where are *who*, exactly? And why don't you let our nurses check on those you've done dirty like that? You know, electrocuted with your non-lethals."

"Bring me the runaway students I'm looking for and I'd be happy to oblige," said the evil twin, signaling a few of the monitors to conduct another town search.

"Even if they were here, which they're not, it wouldn't really be my place to return a naturally free human being to an anti-freedom establishment," said McCoy sternly while conjuring up the fullness of his deep voice. "You know what I mean, 1501, don't you?"

"Tell you what," #1501 shot back, "I'll count to five...."

"Let's make it three," offered McCoy.

"Hmm…" the evil twin nodded. "If the glow doesn't make the students supernaturally appear, well, I'll just shock another Deplorable each and every minute until they do."

People in the crowd gasped. They trusted McCoy with their lives. And for all they knew, the students were well on their way back to the compound. There was no way out of #1501's threat.

"You know what?" said the deputized monitor. "Let's just skip to one."

Nodding to the monitor standing by his right side and pointing at one of the elders sitting toward the front of the crowd, #1501 barked, "ONE!"

"Did you hear that?" asked Joanna, her legs bouncing with energy. "I remember that voice…That monitor from the library! He liked to count. This can't be good, Chih."

"Patience," whispered Nuzrene. "McCoy knows how to handle himself."

The old man fell backwards into the lap of the person behind him. After a loud groan and some violent shaking, the man stopped moving. The shock dart had struck him directly over his heart.

"Hey!" shouted McCoy, tossing his cigar to the ground and walking up to 1501 until they were nearly nose to nose. "You couldn't even fulfill the count? You're being unreasonable. Search the entire property. Take what you want. But you won't find those students, and you won't hurt another member of this community."

"Very kind, McCoy," said the evil twin with a smirk. "I think I'll take you up on that…At least some of it, anyhow."

With another nod, this time to a deputized monitor across the street, the troops immediately dispersed. The townsfolk watched as they turned homes, businesses, and warehouses inside out. Nothing was off limits. Every bit of furniture, clothing, food, and supply was tossed outside. Windows were busted, and doors kicked in, torn from their frames.

When it seemed they were done with their destruction, and no students were found, they moved on to phase two.

"Light it up!" shouted #1501, watching the carnage unfold shoulder to shoulder with McCoy.

Like a scene from an archaic raid, torches were lit using personal items tossed in the streets, then thrown into homes and buildings all around. McCoy stood firm, preferring to watch his office burn, with all the ancient texts, than watch his people suffer any more physical abuse. He helped reclaim this town years ago. He knew he could rebuild it again.

Before he stopped them, a group from the crowd hopped to their feet, running for the firehose stored in a shed nearby. With a nod from their leader, several monitors pelted each of the townfolk with shock darts. Instantly they dropped to the dirt. Face down. Helpless.

McCoy, wide-eyed with clenched fists, started to respond when #1501 shoved a handmade tazing wand into his side. He dropped like a stone. Muscles buzzing and rigid, he was forced to watch, wincing in pain.

Tired of the games, the eviltwin called his troops back to the center of town.

"This outcome is pretty cliche, McCoy. Don't you think?" he whispered, crouching low for McCoy to hear.

Slowly, weeping began to rise up from the front of the crowd.

"You killed him! You tortured an unarmed man!" cried the elder's wife, holding him in her glowing arms. "And for what? To stop the glow? It never ends, does it? Everything you Anti-Libertas touch, you ruin."

McCoy groaned, trying to gain control of his muscles. Trying to condemn the violence with his voice. Sweating and crying, he was completely helpless, a position he swore he'd never enter into again.

Slowly, the deputized monitor rose to his feet. Looking over the crowd he honed in on another group beginning to wail towards the back. Two more townfolk were confirmed dead from his so-called *non-lethal* schock darts. And two more sets of arms and hands began to glow. A glow that slowly spread throughout the crowd.

His stomach turning and his tongue twisted, the evil twin began to sweat profusely, ordering the troop to depart. One by one the monitors disappeared into the forest until only #1501 remained.

With his voice shaking he said to McCoy, "It didn't have to turn out like this…I mean…I never intended… hmph….You have twenty four hours to deliver the students."

By the time the troop had disappeared, the moon was low and bright. Generators had been destroyed and solar panels smashed. Building fires and the glow offered the only light.

13 Hymn Quaking

"**P**raise the glow from the heaven's..." sang the Deplorable, trying to rouse Heschel awake while hoping the glow would carry his song beyond the walls of Compound 40.

"Praise him in the heights above..." he carried on, slowly holding out the final note of each line as if they were the last he'd ever sing.

Mr. Sibyl had learned to sing as soon as he'd escaped Compound 40 years ago. Singing wasn't allowed among the students or staff inside Anti-Libertas compounds. It was, at first, before his time. In fact, The Chamber had leveraged it, enticing creative influencers to wash over the crowds with keywords and approved ideas in exchange for power and privilege. But music is all about expression. It demands and offers freedom. And anti-freedom movements aren't interested in these things. The first time Mr. Sibyl stumbled across a group of people of the light singing together, he was hooked.

And while music among the Deplorables worldwide was easy to come by, the people of the light sang with an honesty and purpose more incredible than anything he'd heard elsewhere. Memorizing as many hymns and psalms as possible, he wanted to fill his heart with song should the day come when the written word once again get canceled.

Like their copies of ancient texts about the glow, most hymns and songs were close recreations. Key names for that supernatural father, the son who put on skin, and the spirit filling lungs and minds, had been nearly lost to history. While Mr. Sibyl knew the lines and poetic phrases, he filled in the blank spaces where titles and monikers used to sit. Like others, he simply called it the glow.

"Praise him, all his guardians, and all the heavenly tribe…" he sang louder, the soundproofing of the hot spot restraining his voice from bellowing down the halls and across the courtyard.

What are you doing? asked Heschel, groggy and gruff. *Is that…singing? Is that how we're supposed to escape?*

Yes… and no, replied Mr. Sibyl, taking a deep breath after belting out that final note. *Yeah, this is singing, or at least one way to do it. But no, we're not singing to escape. We're singing to connect. We're singing because hope can't be contained. We're singing because I believe that escape will come to us.*

Well… it's strange, but I guess it's no stranger than what I've already been a part of. And it doesn't seem too complicated, I guess. Wanna give me some pointers on how to do it? Still weak and lying on his back, Heschel shook his head in disbelief at the unfolding plan.

How about we hum the melody for a start? It's very simple and repetitious. You're a sharp student. You'll pick it up pretty quickly, said Mr. Sibyl before diving right into a vibrant humming of the song.

"Hm, hm, hummm…Hm, hm, hummm…."

After listening through a stanza, Heschel dove in, attempting to copy the veteran singer. Mr. Sibyl was patient. He'd since taught many to sing. But this was different. Heschel's voice bounced from note to note, ahead of the beat, behind the beat, up and down the scale until Mr. Sibyl couldn't believe his ears.

How'd I do? asked Heschel, oblivious to the vocal havoc he'd just unleashed upon his new friend.

Here's the deal, the Deplorable hesitated, graciously navigating through the vocal earthquake. *You know what? Just because a crow isn't a songbird doesn't mean their caws aren't glorious.*

Heschel, quietly resting on his back, was feeling good about his first singing endeavor. Opening his eyes, he smiled at the way it made him feel—at ease and happy for the first time in a long time. He was pretty sure Mr. Sibyl had just knocked his inability to carry a tune but was too enchanted to let it bring him down.

I suppose this'll give me a chance to perfect my skills! Heschel replied, excited to try again.

Singing's all about the heart, Mr. Sibyl gently offered. *How about you just hum along until you catch on? I really believe something magical is gonna burst from our cells tonight.*

It wasn't long after sunset when the two began the ancient experiment. The moon wasn't full, but it was bright. Not that either of them could see it. Back in his flat, Heschel would stare out his window into the night sky, an illuminating reminder that the glow was just as powerful in the dark.

The ancient hymn wound its way through praise and proclamation. They sang about the depths of the ocean and the wild creatures within it. They sang about the power of nature spurred on by the glow's desires. They sang about powerful leaders and impoverished youth, all under the counsel of the glow. And each time they sang a line about the glow raising up his people, Heschel felt his chest burn a little and his stomach turn. At first, he didn't notice the glow radiating from within his throat. But soon, it crept down his arms and into his chest, eventually lighting up the room. Sure, it was an ancient song, but to Heschel, it had become personal. It had become his mission.

They had been singing and humming and crowing for hours. Heschel was just about to press Mr. Sibyl for a break when things began to unravel.

"Do you feel that? Do you feel the ground shaking? It's an earthquake, I'm sure of it!" yelled the Deplorable with wild-eyed excitement. "This is exactly what happened in the story!"

Heschel, still too weak to stand, rolled onto his side, covering his head and neck with his arms. *I feel it. So what do we do? What's supposed to happen next?* He couldn't be sure, but as he rolled over, wondering what was happening, he thought he caught a glimpse of the humanoid glow beside him in the cell. As he did a doubletake, the form was gone.

"Well…I don't know…I guess we wait and see," he said, just as curious as Heschel.

It didn't take long to find out. The ground heaved as it had done in Chagrin and The Adavis Center months before. Only this time, it wasn't contained to a building but seemed to spread across the valley. While the hot spot violently shook, so did the courtyard and the dorms as they crumbled and caved in, and the waterfall on the edge as it widened and deepened, revealing even more hidden treasures, and the forest floor splitting and contorting, and the town downriver already blanketed with destruction.

When it finally stopped, and Mr. Sibyl looked up from the fetal position in the corner, he saw that the door to his cell had fallen with the door frame partially caved in. Heschel's room was the same. And there, standing in the doorway with a shock rifle in hand, was a monitor, clearly shaken and bleeding from his forehead. Lights behind them flickered and flashed. Debris covered their body, turning their brown hair a dusty white.

"I may not be the brightest member of the Anti-Libertas," the monitor muttered, hocking and spitting, their hands trembling, "but I won't be the one to disappoint Chicanery in all this chaos."

The Deplorable nodded, sat back against the wall in awe of the event, then continued softly humming. From the other cell, Heschel joined in.

 **14 The Commissioning**

"They walked cautiously down the main road in the dark, following the glimmer of burning buildings not far off. The smell of burnt plastic, tar, and wood filled the air, making their eyes water and their lungs burn. Even as they finally caught up with the crowd, some still huddled in the street, the haze of thick smoke made it difficult to grasp the extent of the damage.

"What are you three still doing here?" McCoy shouted from behind, his voice firm yet sad. "You shouldn't be here. There isn't time!"

Nuzrene walked over and threw his arms around McCoy. They hugged as the old man shared the names of the two elders and three friends who lost their lives. One of the men had been a close mentor and a father figure to Nuzrene when he first arrived.

Chih and Joanna, tearing up, spurred one another on to action. Splitting up, they joined in to help in the aftermath. Chih jumped on the maintenance crew, working hard in the dark to fire up the generators. They needed to get the water pumps back in full swing. Until then, the fires would continue to spread from one building to the next.

Joanna made it a point to hunt down her roommates. Reassured of their safety, she joined Maria in preparing meals and caring for the families of the deceased. She couldn't shake the horrible thoughts of losing Hesch that roamed her mind.

I can't do this, thought Joanna, scrubbing the same pan over and over. *It's not fair to these people. They're the ones suffering and heartbroken, not me. They need my attention...my compassion...my clear mind. Get ahold of yourself, woman!*

"Woman?" Joanna repeated out loud, weirded out by the sound of it.

"Are you talking to me?" asked Maria, her eyebrows scrunched as though confused and maybe even a little offended.

"You? No! Sorry, Maria," she stumbled over her words. "It's just that...well... it's embarrassing, really. I never thought of myself as a woman before."

"And what did you think of yourself as? A tree? A clump of cells? A lad?" said Maria, cracking a smile to ease her own personal guilt trip. "It's not as strange as you think, Joanna. The Alphabet Coup did a number of us when we were Seekers. You're strange but also sharp and very much a product of the Anti-Libertas."

The evening hours ticked by quickly. The fires were out, and power had been restored haphazardly throughout the town. McCoy had just called everyone to the center of town for a final word of the night when the ground began to shake.

"Is this what I think it is?" shouted McCoy. "Get away from the buildings! Out of your homes, everyone, into the street!"

The shaking rapidly grew into heaving. Those trying to run from buildings were tossed around like kids on a trampoline. Others stayed low, covered one another in the center of town, and kept their heads down. McCoy stood firm like a brave general watching over a field of battle. His joints still stiff from the electric shock, he used every ounce of remaining energy to ride out the storm, refusing to end up in the dirt again.

The sound was overwhelming. Branches breaking and trees falling. Buildings half burned and nearly salvaged from the fire toppled over in ruins. Perfectly fine homes crumbled like sandcastles. Once again, the power went out, only this time with incredible flashes and bangs, like fireworks, which were not so entertaining.

The silence after it ended was startling. No one moved. Everyone seemed to be in shock. First, the Anti-Libertas, and now the land. It was almost too much to handle.

"McCoy! McCoy!" shouted a young man off in the dark nearly a block away. "McCoy! She's still alive! You need to come quick!"

Without hesitation, McCoy took off down the street into the hazy darkness. Tripping over debris and climbing over fallen trees, he followed the sound of the voice.

"Nuzrene? Keep calling out! Turn on your device and wave it in the air—I can't see a thing," he shouted, frustrated by the persistent feeling of helplessness. "Is it Joanna? Maria? Who's hurt?"

"It's one of *them*, sir," he said, somberly helping prop up a young Anti-Libertas monitor half covered in building rubble. "I remember her from the supply chain. She always managed the spreadsheets, you know, double-checking the order. Always kind to us. All of us."

McCoy bent down to check her pulse. Looking her in the eyes, he asked for her name. He never thought to ask her name and never seemed to take notice of her serial number either. She was just another member of the Anti-Libertas. The enemy.

"No   one's…safe…hack-hack…Chamber   is… devouring   everyone…cough-cough…canceling everyone…." Gasping as she struggled to breathe, it was clear she was near the end and just as clear that she needed to speak her mind. "Chicanery…attacking everyone…who disagrees…cough…with the Great… the Great Transition…."

Squeezing Nuzrene's hand while coughing up dust and blood, she violently gasped for air, clamoring for help like you'd expect from someone drowning. Then went limp. Nuzrene, continuing to squeeze her hand, put his head down and began to cry. Six months ago, she might have tried to kill him. But now, at the end of it all, she had recognized the total emptiness of the Anti-Libertas mindset. Nuzrene, like Heschel, knew that without the glow, he could easily have become the next #1501. Or worse.

"Your chest!" McCoy whispered. "The glow."

Sure enough, a red-orange orb of light began to well up behind his shirt. It grew so bright that they were able to see not only the young monitor's face but the faces of two other monitors who must have suffocated beneath the rubble nearby.

"Do you think they were left behind to spy?" Nuzrene wondered.

"No. No, I don't," McCoy said, his voice tender

and low. "I think they were trying to escape the Great Transition…."

"Have you heard about it?" Nuzrene asked, gently laying the monitor down and rising to his feet.

"No. I haven't. But considering the *choices* the Alphabet Coup demanded from people in the past, and those Deplorable people of the light deemed too dangerous to exist…well…it can't be that great. Listen, the lion's on the hunt. Gather the crows—it's time to go."

McCoy rounded up the remaining elders who invited everyone in town to sit in on the final commissioning of the students.

"I'm sorry it has to happen this way, though I'm glad we get to send you off in a proper manner," said McCoy sitting in a circle with two other elders and the three students. "How do those uniforms fit?"

Chih patted the chest of the tight-fitting, drab-gray uniform taken from one of the dead monitors. It was Joanna's idea. They needed a better plan to get to Heschel, and though it seemed morbid *borrowing* the attire of a dead person, she chose to view it from a more redeeming perspective. All three of the young monitors seemed to be risking their lives for freedom, for truth, for a better future. What better way to honor them than to use their resources to further their mission? So, treating their bodies with a divine respect for the dead, the uniforms were removed, cleaned, and put on by the students. And the bodies were placed alongside the others for burial.

McCoy was the first to point it out. The orb appeared at the center of the circle like an orange basketball on fire. The crowd gathering around them in the dark gasped at the sight.

"We haven't seen the glow take on such a distinct physical shape in years," whispered one of the elders.

"More than a decade," said McCoy. "I've never doubted it would return…I suppose it just never occurred to me that I would be alive when it did."

Placing his arms on his crossed legs, palms up, McCoy invited the others to do the same. None of the students had ever participated in a meeting like this. Joanna stared at the orb while Chih closed his eyes, reciting the text he had memorized so far. Nuzrene looked around the circle, finally making eye contact with McCoy as each of their hands began to glow.

"I can feel it working through my arms and into my chest," Joanna whispered. "Do you feel it, Chih?"

"I feel it moving up my neck, relaxing my mind," he said, eyes still closed. "I can picture Hesch. I see him lying on the floor somewhere…maybe The Adavis Center? The re-education room? I see someone else too…the Deplorable? They're being guarded."

The townsfolk murmured as the glow in their palms

formed into tiny flames as if someone had placed a lit match in each of their hands. It flickered and flashed without burning out. One of the elders hushed the audience, calling for a moment of silence before reciting an ancient farewell.

"Compelled by the orb, we now commit you to the power of the glow and to its patient work in the light. A light that will build you up and guide your journey into danger, yet fully confident of your greater mission toward neverending truth. We know the lion is on the hunt and that not only the lion but also wolves and snakes are on the prowl, scouring the land for weak and foolish scraps. We're watchful, and we commission you to go and do great things for the greater good."

The town was silent. The moon was out and bright in the clear night sky. Fog had begun rolling in, and though it brought a chilly air, causing the crowd to cinch their jackets and huddle for warmth, those in the circle nearest the orb remained content.

"We know that in the end, just as those people of the light before have said, it's a greater blessing to give than to receive," said McCoy, his voice firm though quiet.

All six rose to their feet, the orb rising along with them like a chandelier hanging just overhead. Gathered all around, the crowd split in two, making way for the students somberly heading toward the river's edge. As they walked, the people quietly chanted a strangely familiar sound.

"Hoo-hah…hooh-hah, ru-ahh…."

Before long, the orb, hovering above like a shimmering star, multiplied into three flamelike whisps descending to rest on each student. Disappearing from the sight of the chanting crowd, Chih led as they began the slow process of forging a new path through the forest.

 ## 15 Arriving in Style

What took an hour's worth of floating downriver in nearly freezing water required a six-hour hike along the river's edge to return. The sun was beginning to cut through the fog on the forest floor when they arrived at the foot of the waterfall. Right away, Joanna noticed something different.

"Chih, do you see that?" she said, tapping him on the shoulder like a child, the way she did at the sight and smell of blueberry pie for the first time. "The earthquake reshaped the falls. Something's jetting out in the middle, splitting the water in two. It looks like a stone column, doesn't it?"

"So the old maps were right," whispered Nuzrene. "I've scoured the dark-chain for the last year looking for hidden blueprints, campus maps, news articles... Anything that could help us find the so-called hidden library of ancient texts. We know it was here, on this campus, or the one that was here before The Chamber took over. We know this was the last stronghold for ancient documents banned by the Anti-Libertas. It's one of the reasons Chicanery took on the small role of principal here. He wanted to be close. To keep watch."

"I hate to break up a good stroll down research lane," said Chih, "but if Chicanery is as paranoid as we know he is, we ought to keep moving."

"Yeah, I hate to say it, but my leg's pretty well spent," Nuzrene said, leaning against a freshly fallen boulder at the base of the falls. "I haven't pushed my body this hard since I escaped C-21. Since I lost my leg."

"Ummm...Excuse me? Could you repeat that last line? I don't think I heard you right," said Chih, frozen in place and staring at his friend's legs currently in use.

"Which part? Wait, you don't know? I thought it was obvious," Nuzrene said casually.

"What exactly do you mean *obvious?*" Joanna chimed in.

Pausing to let the abrupt news settle in, Nuzrene took a deep breath. "Well, I lost my right leg from the knee down escaping from that Middle-Eastern horror show Chicanery once called the re-education model for the world."

Lifting his right pant leg, Nuzrene revealed a titanium pole joined to a complex mechanical ankle partially hidden by the top of his low-cut hiking boot.

Chih and Joanna sat side by side on a flat sandstone boulder nearby. Their respect for Nuzrene's perseverance and leadership grew immensely. Yet, at the same time, they felt awful about their wild trek along the river's edge in the dark over the last six hours and how painful it must have been for him.

Though Chih had just prodded them to move along, he was unwilling to take another step without some backstory. Joanna shook her head at Nuzrene when he pleaded with them to carry on, promising to tell the story when the time was right.

They refused to budge.

"Key points—okay?" demanded Nuzrene. "According to my infrared satellite imaging app, the next patrol is about ten minutes away. Only the gritty details."

"Wait, wait, wait…You have satellite tracking? Bodyheat imaging? Were you going to tell us?" asked Chih.

Nuzrene smiled, waving at Chih to relax.

"I was a WAFEMA earlier than most. I had just become

an Interpreter when I was given the opportunity to break down and re-educate a few Seekers who had gone astray. I was good at it. So good that the Eastern branch of The Chamber, with Chicanery's direct permission, awarded me the Mature Activator title. I was already a Fully Empowered Wide Awake, regularly consulting with Lieutenant Kresreb on Stream, discussing the latest mind-bending, body-breaking techniques she had been developing in Eastern Europe. It only made sense to promote me."

At the sound of Kresreb's name, the other two students shifted in their seats uncomfortably, nodding as they remembered her sacrifice in the end. Chih threw his arm around Joanna, though neither said a word.

"But over there, Anti-Libertas meant something different," said Nuzrene, looking off into the forest, picturing his childhood home. "In the West, the movement pushed away from ancient law, common sense, created order, and even your rights built in from the beginning—something I've not yet been able to find a copy of on the chain. Even more, it was a mad rush to stamp out the ancient truth about the glow and replace it with self-worship, socio-political tribalism, and divisive theories about everything under the sun. Your leaders tried to erase the past in order to rebuild a utopian dream through re-education compounds."

"And you're saying Compound 21, where you were,

had a different mission?" asked Joanna.

"All Middle-Eastern compounds. With the ultimate permission of Chicanery, they took the language of Anti-Libertas in a different direction," Nuzrene continued, sitting down beside Chih and Joanna on the flat stone. "You see, The Chamber over there despised the Alphabet Coup. They detested their view of progress. Most importantly, however, they hated the glow—the only belief they shared with the West. And it's why finding writings about the glow is so difficult...because everyone worked to burn it all down. Over there, they established their own brand of Anti-Libertas, which they called Fiqh—a word they used to describe the modern interpretation of old surahs, teachings and rules, and ideas about life. Documents we were never allowed to read for ourselves…though I eventually found a way."

"This is the short version?" Chih asked, looking at the time on his device and pursing his lips to contain a laugh. "But how did you lose your leg?"

"Leg? Sorry," Nuzrene said, shaking his head. "I haven't talked about C-21 in a long time. Listen, like you, I found something on the chain. It was a document from The Chamber celebrating our success in brainwashing students with Anti-Libertas reverse-truths. Even more, it went into detail about the next phases of our re-education. It shook me. They called for more severe consequences for students who stepped out of line. What's worse, they demanded that every family member related to a student at C-21 be eliminated. It was the first time I realized I was part of something evil. And I didn't even know what evil was at the time…not by name, anyhow. I felt dirty."

Nuzrene grew quiet. Rubbing his chin, he stared at the waterfall ahead, eventually smiling at its fast-paced yet peaceful nature—a brief reminder of his new life far away from the old.

"My name was on the document," he whispered. "I was ordered to oversee Kresreb's chemical lobotomies… you know…destroying the minds of fellow students who attempted to think for themselves. The brain implants that had been in use for years no longer worked. Students were adapting. Yours and mine and Heschel's. And that's when something happened on the screen. I think you saw it too, Chih. Pixels went wild—flashing and dimming certain words and links. The glow was reaching out, guiding me toward more hidden files, data, information. Truth."

"And you were caught. Tortured. That's how you lost your leg, isn't it?" Joanna blurted.

"Not exactly. My escape went unnoticed at first. Remember the hatch I told you about? The one I regularly snuck through to connect to the chain?" Nuzrene said, rubbing his knee. "Well, I fell down that hatch the night of my escape. I shattered my patella and tore the patellar tendon when I landed wrong. I had dropped into it hundreds of times without a problem. I didn't think I'd make it from there, but by the power and comfort of the glow, I dragged my swollen leg almost painlessly. I crawled a quarter of a mile through the maintenance tunnel, then another mile through the desert to the nearest town, where an illegal, non-Chamber-approved doctor found me. He tried his best to clean my shattered, swollen, torn open, infected mess of a knee, but after days of hiding me in a crawl space from monitors hunting me door-to-door, he eventually amputated it. He saved my life."

"Now here you are, stuck with us on your way back into the danger zone," said Chih, wiping his forehead from the sweat that had formed as Nuzrene described the gritty details of his leg.

"Here I am," repeated Nuzrene, looking at his device as it vibrated. "And here comes the patrol. Time to move into the brush. GO!"

The monitors strolled along the edge high above without so much as slowing down.

Maybe Compound 40 isn't on high alert after all, thought Joanna.

"You two see that? The orb. I've been staring at the hill on the other side of the falls wondering how we're going to scale it before another patrol comes our way. The orb just flashed into existence *right there*, and I think I know why," said Chih, pointing toward an old rope half-buried in the dirt below the glowing ball of light.

"Seriously? It's a big hill, Chih. The glow could be showing you anything," Joanna said, chuckling at the thought of relying on some old, degraded equipment. "With the fog, we don't even know if it's attached at the top. It's practically a death sentence!"

"I won't be able to get up without it," Nuzrene cut in, amazed at the sight of the glow. "It's either that or I walk along the base of the edge until I find a more forgiving slope. To be honest, I don't have any reason *not* to trust that orb, do you?"

Before Joanna could respond, Chih had already started making his way across freshly fallen boulders behind the falls. Once on the other side, he quickly shimmied ten feet up the impossibly steep hill and grabbed hold of the rope. As he did, the orb shot upward, nearly disappearing into the fog at the top of the edge. Holding tight, Chih leaped away from the hill to his right, then back to his left, swinging like a little boy on a vine. Aside from some shifting dirt and a few dislodged stones, the rope held.

"From the look of it, we have about fifteen minutes until the next patrol," said Nuzrene, making his way across the boulders, dirt mounds, and loose sandstone debris. "I'll go last. If I don't make it, at least you two will still have a shot."

"No way. One and the same - the same as one," said Joanna, shocked at how easily the phrase spilled out of her mouth. "Wow! Seems like forever since I recited that."

"It's been years for me," said Nuzrene. "It sort of carries a different weight now, doesn't it?"

"One hundred percent," she said. "We're a murder of crows. We stick together. You'll go first. I'll follow. Then Chih. It's strange, though. I've been so impatient in wanting to embark on this rescue mission, but now that we're doing it, it's like I forget how the glow works. That it almost always moves in the opposite direction I think it should."

"That's what makes it so trustworthy...at least in my experience," said Nuzrene. "Anyone can pull off the normal. But the glow? Always working the impossible and getting away with it."

Joanna smiled at this simple truth. With a boost from Chih, Nuzrene grabbed hold of the rope. While going ahead of the younger students didn't feel right, they were running out of time, and protesting wouldn't have helped anyone. Besides, he had learned the power of female persuasion since arriving in town. Joanna, in particular, could be very convincing when her mind was set.

Up they went, fast and smooth. At the top, Nuzrene stood beside Joanna, watching Chih bring up the rear.

Just as he grabbed hold of the ledge with his right hand, the rope snapped in his left, causing him to swing backward with a thud against the sandstone. Though startling, he was safe. They all were. They had officially arrived at Compound 40.

 ## 16 Like a Flock

Joanna led the way along the edge. It was the same path she had taken with Heschel, Charlie, and Maria during the fall Sojourn. As they passed the small and seemingly out-of-place Microcachrys tetragona, Chih paused.

"If I hadn't followed the glow into your flat or the clues out here to this little shrub…" said Chih, remembering the first time he tangibly experienced the power of the glow.

"The glow had you in its sights, Chih," Nuzrene whispered, patting his friend's back. "And you were searching for the truth. You were curious. And ready.

And I don't know about you, but I've felt a relentless internal tugging since we scaled the edge back there."

Chih nodded, patting his chest and waving Nuzrene onward. Further along the edge, with Joanna still in the lead, they stumbled across an old campsite. It was still there—sort of. The stacked brush pile, the firepit, and the clearing for their tents now hidden by a freshly fallen pine tree. Just as the falls had caused her to reminisce with a heavy heart, she couldn't help but recall leaving Maria right there by the fire only to be betrayed by her on the hill later that night.

"Do you guys remember life as a Seeker?" she quietly asked. "Do you remember how simple things were when you did exactly what you were supposed to do without a single thought of your own? Without decisions? Without options? Without truth?"

"Yeah...I do," said Chih. "I was alone in a sea of students. We may have been an assorted lot from all over the world, but we were the least diverse group on the planet. *Maybe* the externals matter, I don't really know, but it's safe to say that since being awakened by the glow, since really becoming friends...*family*...with you all, and with Heschel...well...look at us! We're not just drab gray, jumpsuit-wearing humans forced to accept The Chamber's cultural reset. We've discovered deep insights about the world and one other, and we keep learning more," he said, glancing over at Nuzrene's leg.

"Because of the glow—which connects us in ways The Chamber of Death could never dream of," added Joanna. "It's why the glow continues to light up one generation after the next, even as the compounds collapse all around us."

Nuzrene stood back, listening to the deep connections the others were making about one another. He remembered having similar thoughts not that long ago. And since their arrival, he was beginning to connect even more dots. Sure their skin and gender and ethnic heritage offered some neat, and in some ways important, differences. How could they not? But they were so much more than that. Their experiences, physical and mental wiring, learned skills, and unique thoughts—these traits not only made them all unique individuals but they helped them function like a body. Different pieces and parts tied together with a singular purpose.

They're right, Nuzrene thought, staring at the fallen tree. *It's the glow. It's only the glow that truly unites us. We have so many excuses to separate ourselves, but Joanna's right—one and the same - the same as one. Of course! Our purpose is to reveal the truth and to trust the glow together as it helps us become the...the anti-Anti-Libertas!* He sighed loudly, the sort of deep sigh you deliver after a deep thought. Turning toward his friends, he was even more emboldened to forge ahead.

"What do you think about all this, Nuzrene?" asked

Chih.

"Well…I think a patrol will be on top of us any second," he said with a smirk. "Let's see if we can make it to the courtyard without any hiccups."

The forest was empty. It always was. Students had a pretty tight schedule, and goofing off and exploring didn't make the cut.

But it was more than just the forest. The outskirts of the main campus were pretty sparse as well. In the past, students would have been training, studying, exercising, fulfilling work duties, or simply moving from one location to the next. Aside from a few small groups in the distance, the grounds were quiet and surprisingly unkempt.

"Chih, it's time to stop slinking. You too, Joanna," said Nuzrene. "We're monitors, right? Monitors don't sneak. They patrol. Let's patrol."

Nuzrene led the way while Joanna fed him directions from behind. As they rounded the first building, preparing to walk between a set of dorms, Chih and Joanna unanimously let out very loud and very startling gasps. Nuzrene would have turned and scolded them had it not been for the dozens of monitors and students at work in the corridor, removing rubble, helping the wounded, and covering gaping holes in the buildings.

Chih? Are you seeing what I'm seeing? asked Joanna,

eyes wide and lips shut tight. She felt the glow flash through her hands and feet. *What happened? Do you think they were attacked? By who?*

The earthquake. The same one that destroyed the town. None of us were spared, said Nuzrene, compassion filling his voice as the glow encouraged his forward motion right through the center of the chaos.

You feel it, don't you? Like we did on the balcony in front of all the monitors and their shock rifles, said Chih.

I don't just feel it, Joanna replied, *I see it. Up ahead! And it's…it's guiding us directly toward the pack of deputized monitors standing in the middle of the torn-up path.*

The glow blinds eyes that see and opens eyes that are blind, recited Nuzrene. *Shoulders back. Look no one in the eye. Let* me *command the way.*

"Who's in charge here?" said Nuzrene, his voice deep, and full, and to the point. "We have information 1501 will find useful."

The deputized monitor in charge stepped forward, looking curiously at Nuzrene. By the look on his face, it was evident he was trying to figure out who Nuzrene was before responding. Chih and Joanna stared straight ahead, ignoring the monitor's looks in their direction.

"It's not my place to rush, but the info is time-sensitive, to say the least," Nuzrene pressed. "No doubt you're up to speed on our little visit to town yesterday? So then, you wouldn't be surprised that those despicable Deplorables have a little something up their sleeve in response. Something 1501 might want to tend to sooner than later, if you know what I mean?"

The deputized monitor stepped back, clearly unconvinced. Wrinkling his forehead, he began staring at Joanna in awkward silence. After a minute, he did the same to Chih. Leaning his head to the side, his eyes opened wide, and he quickly flipped through several pages on his device. Nuzrene, catching a glimpse of the screen, felt a jolt of terror race down his spine. His cheeks flushed, and his knees wobbled.

"Exactly!" Nuzrene shouted, pointing toward the monitor's screen with mugshots of both Chih and Joanna looming large. "You read our minds! We have info on the traitors #1501 won't believe. How did you know?"

The monitor, shocked by Nuzrene's excitement, closed the file and cleared his throat. "Well, then you need to see Chicanery directly. There's no time to waste. No doubt he's in The Adavis Center, harvesting intel from those mutinous traitor's ringleader."

"Can't believe our mighty leader's kept that fool of a student alive after all he's done to upset the smooth education here at C-40. Especially with all that silly magic lighting up the airwaves lately," said Nuzrene, his chest beginning to glow a deep orange, mostly hidden beneath his uniform. As he spoke, the orb above the crowd began to multiply and descend upon the shoulders of not only the three of them but also a handful of other monitors and students quietly at work among the crowd.

Are you all seeing this? Joanna said, her internal voice giddy and nervous.

I don't know whether to be relieved or to assume we're as good as dead. Do you think they can see it hovering over them? added Chih, his heart racing and his palms and feet illuminating even more.

"Looks like we're going straight to the top with this one," Nuzrene declared, stomping his good foot on the ground while saluting the proud monitor before waving his partners onward.

17 Murder Again

The courtyard was equally a mess.

Groups of students were hard at work carrying branches and bricks to designated piles. Some pushed wheelbarrows filled with rubble. Others hacked away the limbs of the mighty oak tree that once stood tall at the center of the courtyard but now lay on its side. The upper half of the tree enveloped a partially destroyed Adavis Center.

Once again, the orb moved ahead of them, multiplying and descending like glowing volcanic globules onto the shoulders of clueless students and monitors hard at work.

"Hey, Nuzrene?" said Joanna, "Any thoughts on the

multiplying orb?"

"Yeah, I do," he said, marching forward before turning to offer a sly smile. "Let the orb do what the orb does best…surprise us."

Without any emotional attachment to the environment, Nuzrene's pace only quickened at the sight of their target. Practically jogging, he beelined toward a gaping hole in the side of the Center for Progress. Chih and Joanna, however, could hardly take their eyes off the devastation. While they hated being back at Compound 40, they were sad to see it so bad off. And the familiar faces of their peers only exaggerated their emotions.

Closing in on the opening, they passed by a student diligently gathering branches, completely oblivious to the sun-yellow orb hovering over their shoulder. Looking up at Joanna, they nodded, flashed a shallow smile, then immediately squinted as though concerned.

The building was dark and empty. The halls were trashed and full of water from the overactive sprinkler system. Knowing a shortcut, Joanna took the lead. After all, neither Chih nor Nuzrene had ever graced those evil halls.

"I've never been to the hot spot, but I'm pretty sure it's in the same wing as the re-education hub," she said, confidently guiding them toward the very room she and Hesch had tried to avoid.

"Do you really think Chicanery is gonna be here?" wondered Chih. "There's so much going on out there, and it's so early in the morning. You don't actually want to talk to him, do you, Nuzrene?"

Nuzrene chuckled, nodding in response. "Chih, you're brilliant on the chain, and your ability to unlock ancient mysteries is incredible…but sometimes I wonder about you."

"What? You told that monitor back there that.…" Chih began to say when it hit him. "Oh…I get it. You were pretending."

The three of them laughed pretty hard as they navigated the crumbling walls and blocked halls.

Making their way to the re-education room, Joanna got turned around several times. The orb, however, continually raced ahead to lead the way until, finally, they stumbled through a smashed wall and into a hallway unquestionably designed for privacy and control.

"Stop! Identify yourselves," a gruff voice shouted from the dark end of the unfamiliar hall. "This wing is off limits. You don't have the clearance. Turn around immediately."

"I was told our supreme leader, the impeccable Principal Chicanery, would be here," said Nuzrene, loud and sharp. "I have vital information about the traitors."

Before the guard had a chance to answer, an explosive

blast of light poured out from Heschel's cell. It was unlike anything Nuzrene had ever witnessed. As if a meteor had crashed to earth and detonated right there in the appropriately named hot spot. Only it happened in terrifying silence.

Nuzrene fell back as the light washed over him, knocking his friends down with him as he collapsed. The monitor standing just outside Heschel's doorless room flew up against the wall, struck by the invisible force hidden within the light.

"Heschel? Heschel! We're coming!" Joanna shouted, breaking free from the weight of Nuzrene on her legs and racing toward his cell as the light faded.

She was nearly there when the fallen monitor reached out, grabbed her leg, and pulled her down with a loud thud and a hard crash on top of the mangled metal door.

Chih was right behind her. Without hesitation, he jumped onto the back of the monitor sprawled out, knocking the wind out of him with a loud grunt. Gasping for air, the monitor waved his hands back and forth in surrender, confused at seeing their C-40 registered monitor uniforms. However, unlike the other monitors and the crowds across the compound, this deputy wasn't persuaded. Recognizing the number printed on the chest pocket of Chih's uniform, his teeth clenched as the shrill sound of a screeching bobcat emanated from his throat. Chih, touching the number tag on his chest, froze, imagining the face of the dead young monitor, covered, and lying in a row of bodies.

Gasping for air in a red-faced rage, the monitor pulled Chih's legs out from under him. Falling beside Joanna, Chih hit the back of his head on the metal door.

"What did you do with my partner?" the monitor growled. "What did you do with the monitor this uniform belongs to? Whose blood is that? Who are you?"

Grabbing Chih's shoulders and shaking, the monitor went crazy, unloading on the young student with a verbal and physical assault none of them were prepared for. Punching, clawing, smacking, and screaming, he went at Chih like a wild cat fighting for its life.

Making matters worse, two more monitors appeared behind the original, each with a shock rifle in one hand and a taser in the other.

Glow…we could really use another blast of help here, Nuzrene silently pleaded. He was about to intervene when the second blast of hot, blinding light swept over them.

Losing his grip on Chih, the enraged monitor, once again, flew through the air—this time violently smacking his head against the hard block wall. The other two monitors were swept up as well, carelessly firing darts that managed to strike both Chih and Joanna. Before hitting the wall, the monitors tased one another midair, passing out cold on the floor beside their twisted-up shock rifles.

"You alright, Ming?" asked Nuzrene, helping Chih to his feet, who then helped Joanna to hers. "You were hit…but not shocked?" he said, completely surprised, pulling darts from Chih's arm and Joanna's back.

"This isn't a normal shock dart. It looks more like a syringe but without liquid," said Joanna, studying the dart before tossing it to the ground. "I don't think their re-education potions work on us anyhow."

"Thanks for having my back, Nuzrene," said Chih, wiping blood from his lip and steadying himself before the three of them turned toward Heschel's cell. "Crows, right?"

"Crows," whispered a subtle, familiar voice from within the cell.

"Hesch!" cried Joanna and Chih in unison. They rushed into the room and dropped to meet their friend on the floor. His hair had grown long and stiff and was matted on the side. And he had the obvious beginnings of a teenage mustache, only with specks of gray throughout, like his hair. The sort of thing that happens to a body under massive amounts of stress.

"I felt it the whole time. I knew it. I knew you were alive," said Joanna, full-on slobber-crying as she hugged her bedraggled friend.

"We never doubted it," said Chih. "The glow wouldn't let us. That low burn just below the surface, sometimes confused with heartburn on this new townie diet and all, but the glow, it never let up. Never let us forget—not even for a minute."

Dehydrated, weak, and wildly emotional, Heschel joined in the crying. He knew they hadn't forgotten him, after all, the glow had already shown him so much. However, even the most steadfast belief can be shaken at the hands of a skilled propagandist like Chicanery. And though he was ashamed to admit it, there were moments he wondered if his friends would ever return for him.

"Thank you…thank you…for not abandoning… leaving me behind," Hesch whispered in halted, snotty breaths.

"I hate to be that guy who ruins a good reunion scene," Nuzrene cut in, "but it looks like those waves of light might have altered our plan for a quiet extraction."

"What do you see?" asked Chih.

"Well, I see a heatwave moving in our direction," he replied, shaking his head at the sight on his screen.

"How many?" Chih followed, beginning to help Joanna lift Heschel upright.

"Well…do you remember all those monitors we passed on the way in? Yeah…that many," he said, stepping forward to take Joanna's place as she struggled to leverage her lack of weight and height in lifting her friend. "And then some."

"Whoa!" exclaimed Chih with a smile. "For a malnourished guy, you're still pretty heavy, Hesch."

The look on Joanna's face let him know the joke had fallen flat.

Hesch smiled.

It was challenging to get him in the right position between them with his arms around their necks, but they managed, and rather quickly too. Joanna had just stepped outside Heschel's cell when the disheveled man stepped forward from the shadows.

"Can I help?" Mr. Sibyl asked.

"Ahh!" Joanna stumbled backward, tripping over her friends and causing them to nearly drop Heschel.

 ## 18 A Deplorable Batch

Mr. Sibyl looked even more wild and unkempt than he had the first time they met at the back of the cafeteria. His hair had grown long and knotty, with a thick beard to match. And both had grayed considerably. His clothes smelled like sweat and mildew and somehow looked even more homely.

While his sudden appearance from the shadows caused Joanna to panic, it was his gentle voice and the sight of the orb hovering over his shoulder that calmed her down.

"I'm sorry…I didn't mean to scare you," he whispered. "I came here months ago to help you two find freedom. Do you remember me, Joanna? The cafeteria? I had to.

And I can't stop. We can't. Not until the lion's hunt is cut short and all crows are free to fly."

"It was you!" Joanna mumbled. "The voice was familiar, and I wanted to believe it was Hesch, but it was you. The Deplorable. You called out to me in that vision."

"Mr. Sibyl," Heschel cut in with a raspy voice. "He's been reaching out for months now."

"My students call me Sibyl."

"Sibyl?" said Chih, under his breath. "Mr. Sibyl? Do you know a short, pretty little woman? Sharp as a thorn? Breathes wisdom and speaks in visions?"

The Deplorable tucked a clump of gray hair behind his ear. His eyes softened even more as a smile cut through his mangy beard.

"We watched a lion attack a bear in the forest," said Chih. "I guess some people know how to follow the glow inside and out because it was obvious we were in the right place at the right time. I would've just seen a predator hunting prey…she saw more. She saw us. Chicanery. People of the light. The hunt isn't over, is it?"

The Deplorable stepped toward Chih and wrapped his arms around him. Looking him in the eyes, he nodded, thanked him, then offered to take his place carrying Heschel.

"Joanna, follow the glow," said Mr. Sibyl. "It'll lead

us to a secret staff-only exit on the side of the building. I found it years ago when I was a student here. Even managed to get through it once…but that was a long time ago. Trust the glow."

"And fast," said Chih. "They're already in the building."

"Which way are they coming?" Mr. Sibyl asked.

"It looks like…well…it looks like my device just died," said Nuzrene, calm as usual.

"Doesn't matter," Joanna said, bold and clear. "We're following the glow…and last I checked, the glow doesn't need our help."

They rapidly navigated the crumbling halls chasing the glow as it dashed this way and that. Heschel's feet barely touched the ground through the darkened tunnels with Nuzrene and Mr. Sibyl quietly at work on either side of him.

The growing sounds of trampled debris echoed throughout the building. The mob was catching up, and with monitors in the lead—monitors who knew those halls forward and backward—the group of Deplorables were beginning to feel the pressure of the hunt.

"They're not after us yet," Nuzrene grunted through heavy breaths. "They're gonna head for the hot spot first. Then the re-education room. Then they'll split up and come for us. It'll happen fast, but we should make it outside before things really heat up."

"He's right," said Joanna. "Lucky for us, I see the glow has stopped up ahead. We've gotta be close."

They had nearly caught up to the glow when the building began to groan. It was like the sound of rusty door hinges being forced open, only huge and deep within the belly of an ancient mansion. They, however, were not in an old mansion. They were in what now sounded like the moaning of a building before it collapsed.

"There's no door!" Joanna shouted, smacking the wall in front of her. "The orb went right through this wall! But there's nothing here."

"We don't have time for this, folks," said Mr. Sibyl. "I don't wanna panic anyone, but in case you haven't noticed, this building is ready for bed!"

"Chih, anything?" asked Joanna, frantically running her hands along the edge of the narrow wall at the end of the hall.

"Well, I could make a joke about being stuck at a dead end…" he said, raising his eyebrows and smiling—the way you do when you've crossed a line.

Joanna glared at him.

"Okay, okay… I'm looking. I just don't see anything," he said, beginning to talk faster. "Guys? Anyone? Sibyl? You've been here before…a little help, please!"

Mr. Sibyl was about to respond when Heschel lifted

his head, turned the palms of his hands toward the wall, and closed his eyes.

"Chih…look," Joanna said, tapping him on the shoulder.

Heschel's palms rapidly began to illuminate. First, a fleshy orange sort of glow, as if an LED were glowing from beneath his skin. But rapidly, it grew brighter, like a white-hot star ready to burst across a night sky. Everyone closed their eyes.

"WHAT'S HAPPENING?" Nuzrene yelled, turning his head to the side as the light was still too bright, even with his eyes closed.

"You're gonna bring the whole building down on top of us, Hesch!" shouted Chih, pressed up against the side wall opposite Joanna, with neither one daring to touch the wall Heschel focused on.

The building shook all the more, and the groaning and creaking grew louder. Their eyes darted all around as the sound of drywall cracking and wood splitting echoed through the halls, freaking them out. The light began to pulse when they heard the sound of a metal latch releasing and old hinges slowly creeping.

It happened fast, within seconds. Heschel, exhausted, once again collapsed into dead weight draped over the shoulders of his friends. The dead end was now a pile of rubble on the floor at their feet. Covered in dust and standing in a hazy cloud, they saw the hidden exit wide open.

"Like I said," Mr. Sibyl whispered, "it was a long time ago."

After making their way through the mysterious metal hatch in the wall, Chih and Joanna pushed the stubborn old door shut. From the outside, the door looked like a section of the exterior wall.

The sun felt good on their faces.

Heschel turned toward the sun. Mr. Sibyl did the same. It had been months since either of them felt the sun's warmth on a beautiful blue morning. While their eyes struggled a bit, the fresh air of freedom, even tumultuous Compound 40 freedom, seemed to rejuvenate their bodies.

"What's that?" asked Chih, pointing high up above the treeline to a slim, wispy, dark mass off in the distance.

"A cloud...maybe some smoke," Joanna said, watching intently.

"It's racing by the other clouds," Nuzrene observed, staring at the mass along with his friends. "It's moving against the wind too. It's coming this way."

"Murder," Mr. Sibyl whispered.

"That's a depressing thought," said Chih. "I didn't take you as a glass-is-half-empty kind of character. We made it this far, didn't we?"

"Of crows," Sibyl continued.

"You think? That would be a *lot* of crows," said Chih, squinting as he tried to block the sun with his hands.

They stared into the distant sky as though the hunt were over. When the hatch had closed, each one of them felt different. The rush that had been pulsing through their veins, pushing them forward like creatures running from predators, had subsided. They felt a peace they hadn't felt since entering the chaotic grounds of C-40.

"Welcome home, Heschel!" The voice roared across the courtyard, loud and confident, like an old friend's greeting after a long trip. The hunt was not over.

 **17 The Great Divide**

Everyone had reason to dread and despise the creature behind the voice echoing through the courtyard. Nuzrene, who, from the other side of the world, was groomed by Kresreb and called by Chicanery to do unspeakable evils to his fellow students. Mr. Sibyl, a former student of C-40, was pitted against his twin brother and forced to choose. Chih-ming and Joanna, his latest obsession, have been hunted and haunted. And, of course, Heschel.

Chicanery's voice bounced off the remaining walls surrounding the courtyard. The way it would at the start of a Sojourn. And just as they were trained as young Seekers, upon hearing their principal's voice, they froze, stiffened their backs, and stood at attention. It was a reflex. And nearly all five traitors succumbed to it—all but Heschel.

"Look at that," Chicanery boasted. "It's part of your DNA! Of course, we knew it would be from the start. Anti-Libertas isn't just a movement. It's a way of life. It's why we rescued you from the Deplorable families you were unfairly bred into. Weak-minded humans guided into desperation by that deceitfully divisive glow."

Heschel kept his eyes on the dark mass up in the sky. Between the power of the glow at work deep within him and his time in the hot spot, very stole his attention. He wondered what his own family was like. He imagined Chih working hard in his hometown and Joanna helping with chores around the house. He knew without a doubt that each of them would have been better off at home. That being raised by their own fathers and mothers would have fostered greater stories for a better future. But he was also thankful to know them and to be with them.

You know Chicanery best, Heschel. What do we do? Nuzrene wondered, keeping his eyes on the old tyrant standing proud on the other side of the fallen oak tree and flanked by dozens of monitors and hundreds of students slowly joining the crowd.

Heschel looked at Nuzrene. *The murder is almost ready. I think the lion needs a little poking first.*

"Do you know me, Chicanery?" Nuzrene called out, shaking the rest of his team from their fear-stricken stance.

"I do," he replied. "You were the most promising re-educator worldwide. The next in line behind Kresreb. Until that deceitful glow lured you into the shadows, where you've been crawling around ever since. With McCoy nonetheless, that decrepit old dog."

"Anti-Libertas is more than a movement, I agree, but it's no way to live," Nuzrene replied, loud and clear, though not shouting. He was never one to shout but instead spoke boldly, like a man on a mission. "The glow chooses whomever it pleases and then truly unifies us. We become family. Members with different gifts, talents, skills, and abilities, and we use them to build one another up without blame or guilt. We're naturally diverse in who we are and how we come together. We don't need anti-freedom committees, or inclusion officers, or demeaning re-education modules. We don't need authoritarian principals and boards claiming progress while denying reality."

"Wait just a minute, young man...student...traitor!" Chicanery stammered as groans and gasps began to rise from the student body surrounding him. "I'm inclusive! Me! My Chamber. My movement. My compounds. My education. *You* defected. *You* abandoned the training. You're an immature Deplorable, like the rest of them.

I alone am the living, breathing definition of truth and justice—and you're either with my utopian vision…or against it. Are you prepared to stand against truth and justice?"

"You've always been a stately communicator, Chicanery," Mr. Sibyl joined in. "I don't know how you do it, to be honest. You could sell salt-water to a fish freely swimming in the ocean. But no matter how hard you try—the glow reignites. You can stomp and smother, mutilate and warp, cancel and oppress…but no matter how dark your world becomes, the glow shines that much brighter. And it scares you, doesn't it?"

Chicanery was just beginning to respond when the small band of traitors heard bangs and crashes on the door behind them. The sounds were random at first, like someone trying to find a handle in the dark. But soon, an incredible clanging began as if a battering ram were charging full-speed at the door from the other side.

Naturally, the group stepped backward, away from the door, and toward the fallen oak in the center of the courtyard. Toward Chicanery. They were surrounded.

It didn't take long before the door flew open and a mob adorned in dirty, gray uniforms poured out. Monitors appeared first. Men and women of all ages, each with a look of determination as they moved to confront the traitors. Students followed behind with the same serious look in their eyes. And they were eerily quiet and controlled, like cats on the hunt.

I'm sorry, Hesch. I thought we could do it. I thought it was time. I thought the glow had something different in mind for us, said Joanna, staring down the mob and slowly stepping in front of Heschel like a mama bear in the face of danger.

"I remember you," Joanna said, pointing out a young lady in front of the growing mob. "I passed by you in the courtyard. The orb was over your shoulder. Don't you see what's happening here? You're free. You're all free. Every one of you. Don't you feel it?"

"Joanna's right. I remember that monitor right there. An orb was over him in the alley," said Chih, pointing to a senior leader in the crowd. "And you," he said, pointing toward a student, "we were in the first session together for years! You can feel it can't you? The glow. It's warm. And it's uncomfortable at first. And it compels you to think on truth and act right."

"Something strange happened," the young lady Joanna called out. "When you passed by, I felt…warm…like Chih-ming just said. Like we knew each other. It's what I imagine friendship might feel like, ya know? Like we read about in past social-deconstruction sessions. Not just partners and people, but friends."

"It's real," said Joanna, squeezing Chih's arm. "It's real, and it's warm."

"But what about the rest of you?" Mr. Sibyl cut in. "Why are you right here, right now?"

"There was a blast," shouted a monitor from the back of the crowd. She was tall, with light brown skin and bright red, tear-streaked cheeks. Her voice was strong yet shaky. "It came from The Adavis Center, and it nearly knocked me off my feet as I led a group of students on the other side of the courtyard. None of them saw it. Or felt it. And then it happened again. Only this time, there was something like a voice within the blast calling me by name…I think. I had no choice. I had to go see what was haunting me."

"Me too," said another. "I was the only one in my group to see it. I had to check it out."

With each proclamation, an orb appeared over their shoulder. As it did, more people were emboldened to speak up, which caused the glowing entity to multiply that much more. Over and over again until a sort of joyful noise radiated upward and outward, overcoming the grumbling welling up on the other side of the courtyard.

I've been waiting for this moment since I escaped C-40 all those years ago. I can't believe it's happening. That I'm here to witness it firsthand, said Mr. Sibyl, encouraging Heschel to stand firm. To trust the glow. To move forward.

I'm with you, said Joanna. *Wherever we go from here,*

I'm in.

So am I, said Chih.

"We're all with you, Hesch," Nuzrene echoed, stepping forward with his arms out like wings, proudly presenting the expanding murder of crows spread out behind him. Without realizing it, he had left Heschel to stand upright of his own volition. And without fail, Heschel stood tall.

Chicanery, shaking with rage, helplessly watched the sizable portion of his re-educated Anti-Libertas body defect to the Deplorables.

"There is no glow. There is no warmth. There is no power." Chicanery turned toward his captive audience, a crowd three times the size of the murder of crows banding together across the way. Staring them down, he calmly began to repeat the phrase, "There is no glow," he would say, then cue the restless mob to repeat. "There is no warmth," he uttered aloud as they copied him in tone. "There is no power!" they repeated, like hyped-up warriors waiting to run to the field of battle.

Heschel, I've provided you with safe spaces your entire life. Do this, and your little flock will fall prey to the hungry lion. It's too late for you, of course, but you can save your friends. Just surrender, and I'll let them all fly free, Chicanery pleaded, heart to heart with the young student, empowered by the very glow he worked to deny.

You know, I saw you in a vision. You were a child. You

connected with the glow once, and it was real back then, wasn't it? said Heschel, staring across the field at the old principal. *It's a mystery to me how you've managed to communicate through the power of the glow like this for so long and yet, with your lips, deny its very existence. You've chosen a different path in your old age. Don't you wonder how far it stretches?*

Immediately after Heschel finished talking, Chicanery lurched forward, bent over, and grabbing at his chest. His face turned bright red, and the veins on the sides of his head bulged like a man under intense stress. As if wrestling with something deep inside his chest, Chicanery lunged backward, ripped open his suit jacket, then shrieked with such pain that the courtyard went silent.

Terrified, #1501 reached out to steady his boss when suddenly the thrashing ceased and a dark mass, like an oily, misshapen orb, protruded from his chest. As bright as the glow was, the black mass matched it in darkness.

"Master Chicanery?" said the evil twin, his knees shaking at the sight of the mass.

It churned like hot tar bubbling outward and defied gravity. In calm disbelief, Chicanery reached up to touch the substance, which screeched and recoiled as his hand drew near. Still gripping Chicanery's arm, the evil twin stepped back at the awful sound. The dark mass popped and pulsed until it finally expelled a tiny spark hidden within. They watched as the light hovered overhead for a moment before dashing across the silent courtyard and uniting with Heschel.

With another violent lunge forward, Chicanery fell to his knees as the tar-like orb withdrew back into his chest, leaving little more than an oily residue on his shirt.

Principal Chicanery stood upright, combed his hair back with his hands, straightened his jacket, then shivered a spine-wrenching shiver as though caught in the snowy-blast of a bone-chilling blizzard.

"Master Chicanery?" whispered the evil twin, barely standing by his side. "What just happened?"

The aged principal turned toward the nervous, deputized monitor. The pupils of his eyes were enlarged, and the color was now black as midnight as if the dark mass had drained them of color. His face was expressionless, while his eyes appeared sharp and piercing. For the first time in months, he seemed focused, like someone finally accepting the cards they're dealt before making a move—a cold-hearted sort of confidence. The kind of person you wouldn't want to mess with.

Turning back toward Heschel, staring straight at him from across the courtyard, Chicanery attempted to communicate mind to mind. Silence. The connection was gone. Only the static hum of a mind emptied of the light of life.

 # 20 Another Day, Another Melee

Chicanery slipped his hands into his pockets, calm and calculated as if ready for an evening stroll along the edge. Without a word, he nodded toward Heschel and the flock of traitors.

"Everyone?" asked #1501.

"Just the students," said Chicanery quietly, with an unsettling smile. "Their immaturity makes them more dangerous…more explosive than our regulated monitors. Unleash them. Let the crows taste the unrestrained emotion of their peers…their fellow students victimized by the very sight of the glow and the grating sound of a Deplorable's voice."

The evil twin lifted his hand high above his head. A dozen WAFEMA Appliers copied him. The loyal students watched intently, beginning to bounce, hoop, and holler in anticipation. Opening his palm, the WAFEMA students once again followed suit. Only this time, and without hesitation, they took off running toward the traitors on the other side of the courtyard. Their loyal peers followed behind.

"Detain them!" shouted #1501. "Remember, they're your flatmates. Your partners in training. Your fellow students. They're blind and deceived, not your enemy...."

Without warning, Chicanery back-handed the deputized monitor across the face. Not a polite, pay attention sort of slap, but a power-driven, backward swing to the front of his face. The monitor's nose cracked loudly, with a stream of red immediately pouring down over his lips and off his chin.

"Tell me…what part of unrestrained emotion did you not understand?" wondered Chicanery, wiping the blood from the back of his hand onto his deputy's uniform.

Across the yard, Anti-Libertas students clashed violently with the newly awakened apostates. It wasn't a well-orchestrated, one-on-one, choreographed type of fight. It was chaotic, like a teenage brawl spurred on by lousy your-mama jokes one-upping and overflowing. It was ugly.

We have to do something, Joanna urged, protected by the newly wide-awake monitors at the center of the brawl. *This isn't how it was supposed to go, Hesch. I… We watched Kresreb sacrifice her life for us in a fight like this. I don't want to see that happen again. Not to anyone.*

Give me your hand, he replied. *Come on, give me your hand. Chih, take her other hand. You too, Nuzrene, join the circle. And Sibyl, grab ahold.*

"Umm…Hesch? Are you feeling alright? We're, like, getting clobbered here, and you want to huddle up in a happy place?" said Chih, reaching for Joanna's hand while using his backside to help support those encircling them. With a look of disapproval, Joanna took Chih's hand. With a wink and a smile, he grabbed Nuzrene's hand.

As soon as the five of them locked hands, an orb descended upon their circle. As it lowered, it expanded like a bubble rapidly being pumped with air. The orange membrane spread out further and further until all five of them were inside a dome-like structure—thin enough to see through but thick enough to muffle sound on the outside.

Nuzrene and Mr. Sibyl looked at one another with wide eyes, ducking as the orb expanded.

Heschel, what about the others? Mr. Sibyl asked.

Crows of other flocks, right?

Heschel let go of their hands and stepped toward Mr. Sibyl. Though chaos had erupted all around them, he was smiling. A gentle smile. The kind of smile a father shows that says everything will be okay.

You're a kind man, Mr. Sibyl. I wouldn't be here if it weren't for your faith and action, Heschel said, squeezing the shoulders of the brave Deplorable. *But this next part is for us to work out. Go on and reach out. Grab ahold of one of our newly awakened people of the light. Grab ahold of them and pull them into the orb alongside us.*

But look at them, said Joanna. *They're entangled with all the other students. It's a mess out there. How do we grab them without getting hurt? Look at 'em...they want to destroy us!*

You'll see, Heschel replied. *Do you trust me, Joanna? I trusted you to return for me, and here you are. This is our journey. We're still in this together. Crows, right?*

Upon seeing the strange glowing dome form around the very students he wanted to see dead, Chicanery nodded again. The evil twin raised his fist in the air without question. Leading deputized monitors in the crowd copied his action.

"Lieutenant Sibyl?" said the principal, as calm as ever. "There's no reason our monitors should get their hands dirty. Let's not be too selective with our shock darts."

"You're saying they should fire on the whole crowd?" the evil twin asked reluctantly, holding gauze from his medical pouch over his broken and bloodied nose. "On our compliant students as well?"

"I imagine it sounds unnecessarily evil—something a wicked, warlord, tyrant would have done during medieval times. Hmm. When I was a foolish child, I was forced to memorize the saying, 'With great power comes great responsibility.' Well, I have the power, and it's my responsibility to use my cogs in my machine however I see fit. Say it with me, 1501—progress before people."

"Progress…before…people," repeated the deputized monitor under his breath.

Calling out the orders, more than a hundred monitors loaded their shock rifles with fresh cartridges, repositioned themselves to encircle the brawl, and waited for the command to fire.

Holding his device close to his lips, #1501 counted down from five.

"Five. Hold steady."

"Four. Bend your knees and breathe."

"Three. Take clean shots. Don't waste your darts."

"Two. Remember…you were students like them once."

SMACK!

Before he could turn away, #1501 took another crack

across the face. This time, however, his device, which he had been holding close, smashed into his cheekbone and eye socket with horrifying power. Chicanery didn't hesitate, as if he was prepared for the sympathetic monitor to wimp out.

"FIRE!" Chicanery shouted into his device while watching his sidekick collapse unconscious.

As the countdown descended, something strange happened to Heschel within the glowing dome—he began to morph. With each number called out, the fiery glow consumed his body more and more until, at last, he fully appeared as the glowing humanoid figure he had interacted with in the library months before. He hadn't become that figure, only *like* it. He was still very much Heschel, only now slightly matured and glowing. Again.

 # 21 With or Against

It was an eerie sight from the rooftops. A rapidly expanding illuminated dome consuming everything and everyone caught in its path.

At first, it appeared as if the lava-like dome swallowed up only those students with a flame brightly hovering over their shoulders. But it wasn't long before others were consumed as well. And once inside, some immediately went to work rescuing their peers. Others, however, appeared dazed and confused, safe but unsure.

"Umm…1501? Are you there?" The monitor stationed atop the remains of Chagrin Center ceased firing in hopes of gaining clarity on the wild events below. "1501? Are you aware of the giant orb…or bubble-blob forcefield… whatever it is, do you see what's happening down there?"

Of course, Chicanery was watching it unfold. Standing on the trunk of the fallen oak, he had drawn as close to as possible without being in the line of fire.

"You're either with me or against me," Chicanery replied to the nervous monitor. And in true Chicanery showmanship, his reply was intentionally broadcast to every monitor on the firing line. Everyone would have to decide if they were worthy of inclusion in the future of the Anti-Libertas movement…or if they were simply Deplorable adversaries of it.

It was a fantastic sight, really. Had Chicanery not rejected the last bit of light in his life, he might have been impressed or at least terrified. Instead, he stood motionless. Hands in pockets. His eyes darted back and forth across the battlefield as loyal students succumbed to fistfights, shock darts, and even the expanding orb. And while his obedient students far outnumbered the traitors, they rapidly diminished in number and strength.

Dead-center within the dome, Heschel orchestrated the expansion. Twisting and turning in every direction, he continuously called out which students to engage just outside the glowing boundary line. As he did, someone from within the dome would reach through the illuminated wall and grab, wrestle with, and hold fast to whomever Heschel pointed out. Sometimes it was a

quick shoulder grab and a pull to bring them to safety—
other times, it was a full-on fist-swinging, bloody-nosed,
ripped-uniform brawl.

The orb expanded in leaps and bounds. It moved fast,
though uneven. One side pressing forward for a time,
then another, and another. It looked more like a giant,
radioactive amoeba than a shield. All the while, shock
darts rained down haphazardly, temporarily paralyzing
every poor soul who happened to get in the way.

At first, monitors aimed the dome hoping to neutralize
the source of the problem. Had #1501 been awake,
he might have steered them away from such a plan.
Considering what he witnessed in the museum months
before, it was clear darts had no effect on Heschel and
only seemed to bolster his strength and immunity. That
said, many cartridges were wasted before they began
firing solely on the mob outside the dome.

Don't worry about those shocked by darts, Heschel
noted. *When they wake and find themselves within this
bizarre bubble of protection, they'll either freely join in
the light...or reject us and escape. The choice will be
theirs, not ours.*

"Why are some resisting, Hesch?" Chih yelled as he
grabbed the arm of a monitor just outside the dome. "Like
this one! Why is he resisting...when... it's so obvious the
glow is with him, hovering over his shoulder?"

The orb is just a taste, said Hesch, recalling something he'd read months ago on one of the short, translated scraps left in the box hidden in their flat. *When you saw the glow for the first time at work on your computer screen, you got a taste of its power and a glimpse of its existence. You didn't yet believe it. You didn't trust it. Well... they're the same way. They see it, feel it, know it's right in front of them... but they don't yet believe it.*

"Shouldn't we just leave them alone, then? Let them figure it out?" asked Chih, stepping back from the chaos to catch his breath. "Shouldn't we let those who want in to jump in and let the rest go down with the ship?"

When a man's drowning, thrashing about, and choking on water... do you row a boat close enough to give him hope and then just stare and wait? asked Hesch, his internal voice soft and gentle, almost whispering, yet crystal clear in the chaos. *Or do you also dive in and wrestle him to the stern, throw his arm up to grab a brace, and give him a chance to catch his bearings? Then, if he prefers the wild waters, that's on him. The glow's already reached out. Now we're gonna give them a chance.*

"Like my brother and me when we were young," said Mr. Sibyl, laying a wounded monitor down in the grass away from the dome's edge. "We both saw the light. Each of us interacted with it in our way. And each of us chose."

They were exhausted. Joanna, Chih, and Nuzrene had been awake for more than twenty-four hours and hard at work the whole time. Whenever it seemed the hunt slowed down across the courtyard, another wave would arrive with escalating rage and despairing contempt for those within the dome. And when the Deplorables' bones ached, or their muscles tightened, or their mind wandered, the glow would reignite them. A fresh wind would fill their lungs, and a surge of hope would overcome them.

Soon the monitors that had been shooting darts from a distance began to enter the fray with clenched fists and sturdy boots. For every monitor whose heart softened, with eyes that began to shine in curious wonder about the glow—nine more would sharpen their vitriol for those abandoning the Anti-Libertas faith. The whites of their eyes would turn red while the color seemed to ooze from their iris'. Spittle and foam would build up along their lips as they growled and shrieked at those within the dome.

Like wild animals caught up in the hunt for the sake of the kill, they began to claw and scratch at the ever-expanding forcefield.

"Brother?" whispered Mr. Sibyl, peering through the orb past several wild-eyed students growling at him through the orange glow.

"Did you say something?" Nuzrene asked, pulling

another student, now awakened by the glow, into the dome and out of the claws of a small band of hunters.

"I think I…I think I saw my brother…wounded..." he said, his words trailing off as he shimmied side to side for a better view of the far side of the courtyard. "It's him…back there…just standing and watching from a distance…and he looks hurt."

"Yeah, that's him alright…" agreed Chih, sidling up to Mr. Sibyl to catch a glimpse. "He's a nasty one. I've been on the ugly end of his reign of terror."

"Me too," said Mr. Sibyl.

"Really?" Chih asked, stepping over a monitor sprawled out on his back, knocked out from the shock wand of a menacing monitor.

"Who do you think oversaw my confinement in the hot spot these past few months?" he gently replied, his voice wavering at the thought. "I'm going to him."

"You're what?" exclaimed both Chih and Nuzrene in disbelief.

"I've been in worse situations," Mr. Sibyl asserted, building his courage.

"You've encountered something worse than a field filled to the brim with rabid, brainwashed, dead-eyed hyenas on the hunt for you and eager to drag your dismembered carcass before The Chamber?" Chih wondered aloud with arms outstretched, pointing to the pack of beasts beyond the bright orange veil.

"Well…maybe not exactly like this," Mr. Sibyl shot back with a smile before saying, "I'll be back," and disappearing into the mob.

"Hesch!" yelled Chih. "He's gone! Mr. Sibyl's left the…the…whatever this is! He's gone to see the evil twin. Stop him!"

Heschel turned to see Mr. Sibyl jog across the courtyard. Without a word, he returned to work helping rescue others from the hunt.

The evil twin nervously watched as his Deplorable brother ran toward him through the battlefield. Not long ago, he might have tased him before letting him utter a word. This time, however, he wasn't so sure his brother was the evil foe he believed him to be all these years.

"You look good," said Mr. Sibyl, coming to a stop several feet away. His voice was jolly, with a smile as big as ever.

"A twin joke?" said Lieutenant Sibyl. "We haven't spoken in years, and you start by giving yourself a compliment?"

Mr. Sibyl's smile grew. "You don't have to…."

"Don't. Don't do this. I'm… I'm responsible for all this," said the evil twin, motioning to the brutality around them. "When I watched that dark mass expel the last spark of light from Chicanery, I knew right then…I knew I had been on the wrong side of everything."

Mr. Sibyl stepped forward, standing arm's length away now.

"Don't. Don't come any closer. Don't touch me," said #1501, holding his hand up and looking away from his brother. "I can't imagine what you must think of the person I've become. I don't want to know."

"Do you remember when we first arrived here? Marched into The Adavis Center. Numbered. Outfitted. Sent off to our first flat without a meal after days of travel," whispered Mr. Sibyl, cheeks red and eyes watering. "Mom told you to look after me…so you did. Only a couple of minutes older than me, but you listened to her like a big brother. That first night you refused to let me sleep alone, even though you were ordered to. You curled up next to me. I never thanked you for that."

Lieutenant Sibyl wiped his good eye, the other one having swollen shut after Chicanery's final blow. Without looking at his brother, he reached forward, grabbed him by the arms, and pulled him close. They both wept.

"That's enough," said the evil twin, clearing his throat with a grimace. "I'll create a distraction. Some people think I'm still in charge around here…for the moment, anyhow."

"You're coming with us," demanded Mr. Sibyl.

"Of course, I'm not," he said matter-of-factly. "You'll

only have a couple of minutes before the smoke clears. Use it wisely. And use that crazy shield as long as you can…at least until you reach the edge. After that, I can't help you."

Mr. Sibyl didn't argue. He didn't understand his brother's decision not to run, but he knew he wouldn't change his mind either.

"Thank you," mouthed Mr. Sibyl before turning back toward the center of the chaos.

Lifting his fist in the air, #1501 hit the siren call on his device. It was a standard call to attention channeled throughout every device connected to Stream on C-40. Within seconds every student and every monitor loyal to Chicanery stopped what they were doing to await instruction.

Fights along the perimeter of the dome continued for several minutes until the remaining traitors took their chance to enter the protective orb.

Before Chicanery could stop him, #1501 shouted, "Smoke them out!" Without hesitation, each monitor removed their two standard issue S18 smoke grenades, pulled the pin from the first one, then tossed it. Having trained for moments like this, they knew to wait approximately ninety seconds before discharging the second canister, leaving room for the smoke of the first to clear and orders for the second.

Mr. Sibyl had just made it to Heschel when the first grenades were discharged.

"My brother!" Mr. Sibyl shouted, leaning on his knees, panting. "It's a distraction. We need to go!"

Without debate, Heschel made his way to the edge of the orb, communicating with everyone inside the dome. *You have the glow now. Each and every one of us. Trust it. We're crows. Trust each other and stick together. Now follow Joanna!*

Just as quickly as the smoke covered the field, the murder of crows disappeared. The dome dispersed as they ran, breaking apart into dozens of smaller orbs that darted across the massive moving crowd and uniting with the shimmering spheres already hovering over each of the new crows.

Racing toward the edge, Joanna led the new troop in a roundabout way across the grounds, behind buildings, carefully through the rubble, along narrow walkways, and ultimately to the edge. Once there, they jogged in silence with only the sound of a couple of hundred feet crunching debris on the forest floor.

From their own devices, the Anti-Libertas-turned-Deplorables listened as #1501 ordered the deployment of the second round of smoke grenades. His simple diversion worked despite Chicanery's attempt to call them off.

Seconds later, they heard another unsettling sound. Crows, a lot of them, cawing as they descended into the smoke in the courtyard. The cawing was immediately followed by the youthful screams of terrorized students and the shouts of monitors calling for runners to bring out live ammunition. Screaming and gunshots echoed throughout the forest and along the edge well after the smoke had cleared and the unexpectedly large flock of Deplorables had safely arrived at the falls.

"Nuzrene?" called the familiar voice from the other side of the crowd.

"McCoy? Is that you?"

"Haha! I can't believe this," McCoy said, laughing at the size of the crowd now making their way down the steep hill with ropes and help from members of the town. "Did everyone make it back?"

Nuzrene nodded. "We made it…but it wasn't pretty. It wasn't what we expected."

McCoy grabbed the young man's shoulder and squeezed. Nuzrene had never seen him look so energized and encouraged. So many people freed from The Chamber's relentless control. And all at once. He'd never seen anything like it. Ever.

Heschel, Joanna, and Chih caught up with Nuzrene, shared hugs all around, then stood still, staring into the forest behind them, listening to random gunshots ring out from the distant courtyard.

"I think you've managed to wake the bear," Mr. Sibyl interrupted, joining them in their watch party. "And, at least for now, put an end to the lion's hunt."

"It doesn't seem like…an end…you know?" Chih stammered, searching for the right words.

"It's not the end, that's for sure," Heschel replied. "But I can only imagine Chicanery's leadership in The Chamber and at Compound 40 will be called into question by other Anti-Libertas leaders worldwide. Maybe crows aren't the end of him. Maybe it won't be the bear. Maybe it'll just be another lion on the hunt."

"Lady and gentlemen," said McCoy, quietly appearing behind them, "It's time. You're the last to hit the ropes. I'll follow behind this time."

Against his desire, Nuzrene went first, humoring Joanna, who stood there with a humorously sinister smile.

Mr. Sibyl followed closely behind, fully entrusting the students' safety to McCoy and eager to reunite with his wife who was currently assisting the wounded at the bottom of the falls.

Joanna, Chih, and Heschel stood at the top beside the rush of water.

"It feels different this time, doesn't it?" said Joanna, looking out over the valley below.

"It looks different, too," added Chih. "You know... after the earthquake you apparently sang into existence!" Laughing, he elbowed Hesch in the side. The others chuckled as well.

"It wasn't such a beautiful sky the last time I was here," Hesch said, bringing a little weight to the moment. "And I must have put you two in a pretty tough position the last time you stopped here."

"How do you suppose? I mean, it was you who sacrificed for us," said Chih, kicking pebbles over the ledge and glancing at Joanna. "You rescued us. And I left you behind. Though, I'm not sure I would have made it in the hot spot like you and Mr. Sibyl."

"It wasn't your fault, Hesch," Joanna added. "And it wasn't yours either, Ming. We probably wouldn't have jumped if it had been up to me. I couldn't do it. I couldn't sacrifice the way Hesch did."

"How touching. I always thought you to be a little more decisive under pressure, Joanna," declared the man now standing directly behind them. "I thought you'd make a great WAFE. Of course, that was before you became a re-education denier anyhow."

The students turned around, standing face to face with Principal Chicanery.

"You'll have to apologize to Mr. Sibyl for me. His brother won't be joining him. In fact, he won't be joining anyone. Ever." said Chicanery with an empty laugh that echoed through the valley.

The students stood in silence. There was nothing to say. Without an ounce of light within him, Chicanery felt no remorse for what he was about to do. While he was willing to abuse them, even destroy them, he had always acted despite the misgivings within his conscience. Now, however, that little voice deep within was gone—dead in the courtyard. And his empty eyes showed it.

Chicanery pointed his shock pistol directly at Heschel. "Hold hands," he coldly commanded.

They obeyed. Holding hands was a comfort they were never afforded as students of Compound 40. But now, even if it meant they'd all experience the painful bite of the shock dart, at least they'd be together.

"Who knows?" Chicanery snarked. "Maybe the glow will help a few Deplorables catch you down below when your legs give out?"

It happened fast. The mechanical sound of the trigger. The micro-combustion of the firing mechanism. The release of the shock dart. Even the sound of it whipping through the air.

Chicanery hit the ground like a felled tree. His limbs twitched as his body shuddered. Gritting his teeth and groaning uncontrollably, he was entirely immobilized.

"You know," said McCoy, walking out from behind a

copse of trees nearly twenty feet away, "I never really liked him…and I definitely didn't trust him."

The students looked back and forth between Chicanery and McCoy. Butting their heads together in a semi-circle, they laughed. It was one of those deep, infectious belly laughs that bubble up when no other response will do. They weren't laughing at Chicanery, their latest near-death experience, or their hand-holding. It was simply the overflow of a season of chaos, wrapped in joy, and released in the free expression of laughter with friends.

"What now?" Hesch asked McCoy, gaining composure.

"We go home," he replied, walking towards the edge and waving them ahead.

"But…Principal Chicanery…We can't just leave him, can we?" Chih blurted out.

"McCoy's right," said Hesch. "It's time to go. If we take him, imprison him, interrogate him. We'll get nothing."

"Except endless attacks by the Anti-Libertas cultists who would do anything to get him back," Joanna proclaimed.

"Exactly. And to be honest, it isn't just his conscience and character that have decomposed—his hold as king lion is pretty weak too," said Hesch. "Who knows how many progress-minded tyrants in the making will be hunting him down."

Hesch watched as the others descended the line. McCoy wouldn't leave until all three had hit dirt at the bottom. Before he left, Hesch, with his chest softly glowing, slowly made his way to Chicanery's side, knelt, then whispered, "I want you to know something I've thought a lot about lately. I think your grandparents would be crushed to see you now. But...but I forgive you."

Chicanery's eyes widened. His lips curled. Drool oozed from the corner of his mouth. An awful noise, like a wounded dog growl-whining in pain, emanated from deep within him. It was both horrifying and emboldening. And McCoy and Heschel were confident that a colossal change had come. That in their little town downriver and everywhere the Anti-Libertas movement had once infected, light was dawning.

"I heard whispers about a light-filled, humanoid figure appearing and even connecting with you a while back," said McCoy, looking out over the valley with a hand on the student's shoulder. "Heschel, I want you to consider joining the elders and me in town. Seems you've been chosen for something a notch beyond your years."

"I think we just accomplished that task, don't you?" said Heschel, his voice soft with a hint of concern. "Whatever I might have been chosen for is over now, isn't it?"

McCoy took a deep breath, smiled at the young

leader, squeezed his shoulder, then held up the rope for Heschel to begin his descent. "Chicanery's downfall is an impressive feat…that's for sure. But a powerful man is only part of the story. The ideas that spurred him on are still out there destroying families and communities… even among us Deplorables within our petty arguments over resources and rights. We need a…."

"Torchbearer," whispered Hesch, cutting in on McCoy's monologue. "A messenger for the next generation from an ancient source."

Epilogue: The Approval

"They answer yet?" Joanna asked, chopping the overgrowth blocking the narrow path outside of town.

Heschel smiled. He knew she couldn't wait five minutes without asking about it. "Yes."

"Yes, we can go?" she exclaimed.

"Yes, they answered," he replied.

"So it's a no then," she declared. "If it were a yes, you'd have just agreed with me. It's always a no. And you always draw it out. This is exactly what it felt like when we were waiting to snatch you up at the compound last year. And yes—this is me being patient, thank you very much."

Joanna hacked away at the innocent ferns and fast-growing red-twig dogwoods lining the path.

"I'm not sure we need to widen the path, J," said Heschel, chuckling at the intensity of her patience.

"I need a little space here!" she yelled back. "Is that a problem?"

"Yes."

"Tough!" she yelled, slashing her way forward without looking back.

"I said yes," he repeated. "It's approved."

The forest grew silent, except for the cawing of a handful of crows perched high above. Off in the distance, the sound of construction echoed from town while the growl of motorboats working the river came and went.

Joanna turned to face her friend. She had the look of a person who was not in the mood for another prank. The look of someone demanding a straight answer before things turned ugly. Uglier when a machete was involved.

"The four of us have their blessing," said Heschel, not intimidated by her demeanor. "We can leave once we have a clear game plan and the right supplies."

Joanna skipped toward her friend, laughing in short bursts of disbelief.

"Whoa! Drop the sword first, please!" he yelled, stepping back with his hands up in protest.

Without missing a beat, she dropped the immense

knife, smashed into him, then squeezed tightly. "It's gonna take some time to prepare. Of course, it is, but it's happening! I can't believe it's finally happening! Wait… you just said the four of us. Who else? Of course, Chih, but I didn't think anyone else wanted to go. Do they think we need a babysitter?"

"Let go…I need oxygen…too tight…" he whispered, peeling her arms away.

"Sorry."

"Nuzrene."

"Nuzrene? I thought he was sticking around to continue developing F.I.L.L.?" she wondered, immediately excited at the thought of him joining.

"Yeah, well, it looks like he's further along in developing the Fellowship of Individual Light and Learning—*not sold on the name yet*—then we realized," Heschel said, rubbing his hands together and nodding.

"You don't sound too excited about it," she noted, picking up her machete and wiping off the green sludge on her shorts.

"I couldn't be happier, to be honest," he replied. "It's just that there are so many new students here that need so much attention. I mean, you guys spent several months with Nuzrene in class every day. Discussing ideas. Uncovering truth. Sharing life, faith, and wisdom. What about them?"

"They'll be fine," she said, spitting on the blade and picking at the stubborn sap. "They'll have the elders and the whole town. They'll be busy. And most importantly… they have the glow. I've never seen the glow so active in so many people all the time. It's incredible, really. And it needs to spread if we have any hope of turning the Anti-Libertas tide."

Heschel nodded. He knew she was right. She usually was.

Stepping past her and moving up the trail, Heschel got back to work, clearing the path. It wasn't hard work, but it was the first round of trail cleaning after winter, with the new spring growth out in full force, along with plenty of fallen branches from the hard winter.

"Do you think we'll find any of them?" Joanna asked after several minutes of steady chopping.

"I think that's a new record," said Hesch, busting out laughing.

"What new record? My work pace? Chopping abilities?" Joanna barked, lunging at the shrubs closing in on her.

"Your silence," he stated matter-of-factly.

"Ugh."

"Yeah," he said. "I do."

Return of the Guide Series

The EDGE: Book One   The CHAIN: Book Two

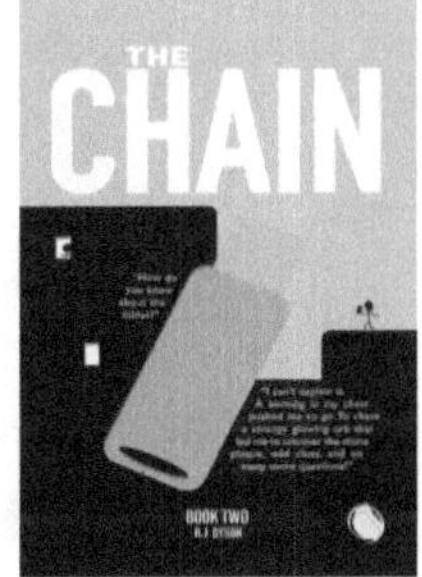

Book Two Web Short:
0561 Downriver

(Follow the QR Code below to download.)

www.ingramcontent.com/pod-product-compliance
Lightning Source LLC
Chambersburg PA
CBHW032012120726
47902CB00014B/2091